DEATH BY ASSOCIATION

BY: KATHLEEN D. RICHARDSON

Acknowledgements

First off I would like to extend my deepest love to the one and only man that has stuck by my side no matter what. He has never judged me and has loved me unconditionally. And that's my Lord and Savior Jesus Christ. I cannot do anything apart from him. He has been a friend when there wasn't anyone that was willing. I'm forever grateful and humble.

Secondly I want to thank my parents for all their love and support. If it wasn't for you guys I wouldn't be here. Thank you for always praying for me. My hands will never stop working because of the things that you all have installed in me. I love you.

I thank my loving husband of five years. We've been sticking together like glue since high school over 18 years ago. Thank you for always sticking by me no matter what. I know what true love is and it's because of you. You have given me two beautiful children whom means the world to me. Shout out to my two knuckle heads. I also want to thank my sisters/brothers for always being there for me and encouraging me through this journey. *Who needs besties when you have sisters!*

Last but not least, I want to thank Denora Jefferson Boone for giving me a chance on this new embark in my life. *I'm forever grateful.* #AIP

Websites: Inspiringdevotions.blogspot.com/ Facebook: Author Kathleen D. Richardson/ Twitter: @AuthorRKathleen

www.AnointedInspirationsPublishing.org

www.facebook.com/AnointedInspirationsPublishing

Instagram: @anointedinspirationspublishing

Twitter: @A_I_Publishing

Synopsis

Growing up Claudia was always overlooked. Being young,

afraid, and alone can lead you to look for attention elsewhere.

Her Mother was the root cause to all of her pain and struggle.

There were times she tried talking to God but it seemed as

though he was never available. When Claudia befriends the

wrong people, it causes her life to go downhill faster than she

could have ever imagined. The only choice she had was to take

matters into her own hands. Claudia finally realizes that she

must turn her life around before it's too late. Will God finally hear her cries, will she be left alone once again, or will the

people that she allowed to get close to her cause her death just

by their association?

Prologue

Ever heard the saying, "You are what you eat?"
Different types of foods that we consume can make us sick. It
can even cause serious health problems. We get high blood
pressure, high cholesterol, diabetes, and so forth. So, one day,
we decide we don't want to eat unhealthy any longer. We start
to exercise and watch what we consume. As we keep this up,
we start to feel healthier, stronger, and much lighter, because of
all of the bad foods that we stopped consuming on a daily basis.
If we continue to eat badly, we know that, eventually, it will
kill us. What about the company we keep, places we go? Can
they be just as deadly?

Who would have ever thought that a small town misfit,
hooker, and dope dealer from Tennessee would end up a small
town hero? Coming from an abusive home to the streets of
abuse, you would have thought that there was no chance for

someone in her position. But, the power of God can take you places you have never thought. Being molested and raped at a very young age, and holding it inside, can really take a toll on you, but coming from where Claudia came from, it wasn't something her family talked about. She tried talking to God so many times, but it seems as though he wasn't interested, either, so she starts to numb the pain the best way she knows how... sex and drugs. Anything to ease the pain for a little while, right?

After that stops working... what's next? Being the middle child was never fun. Claudia was looked over and was always blamed for everything. Her oldest sister, Melissa, was the smart, gorgeous child who always got her way. You know, tall, thick in all the right places, long flowing hair. Everyone wanted to be her. Her youngest sister, Iyanna... well, she was pretty much good at everything. Her mother's "favorite." Growing up, things were okay, but only when her mother was sober and that was only about five percent of the time. All she

knew about her Dad was that he was never there. Living in a

small town, where everyone knows your business, was never

easy. There was never anything to do, but pretty much get into

trouble.

CHAPTER 1

His warm and slimy body crept into my bed. I could feel his breath upon the back of my neck as his hands felt upon my leg, but the fear that plagued me would not allow me to move. I just couldn't understand why my mother's boyfriend was in my room, on my tiny mattress, touching me. I closed my eyes for a second, wishing and praying that I was dreaming, but, I wasn't. That was a real life nightmare. The tears fell from my eyes onto my pillow, and my heart began to race, as he slid my Mickey Mouse underwear from my body. I yelled, and I cried for my mother, but she never came.

"Help, help." I yelled, as I tried pushing him away.

"Shut up! Shut up!" He yelled, as he held one hand over my mouth, while unbuckling his pants with the other.

He was stripping me of my innocence, while my very own mother was in the next room high on drugs. My bed was wet with blood after he finished doing his business. As I sat in my bed, rocking back and forth, I cried and wondered why anyone would want to hurt an innocent ten-year-old. I couldn't understand why the very place that was supposed to be safe, wasn't. He threatened to kill me and my sisters if I told anyone, so I held it all in, not mumbling a single word. My sisters were the only people in the world who I knew that, for sure, loved me. I couldn't risk losing them.

The next morning I was stiff, and I could barely move. I laid in my bed and watched the floor and walls, as the roaches passed by.

"Hey, little buddy. I sure wish I was you right about now," I said, as I watched it crawl up my mattress.

I needed someone to talk to. It was the summer, and my sisters were on summer vacation with their dads. Melissa's dad

would always offer to take me, but my momma never allowed.
The only reason she allowed my sisters to go with their dads
was because it was court-ordered. One time, child protective
services came by the house, because Melissa's dad reported
her, but just like a dope head, she stayed on her toes when her
dope money was on the line. She made sure that the house was
clean and the fridge was full. She made sure that she wore her
best outfit and made up her face. Whatever she had in her
system was gone with just a swallow of a pill, cleaning her
completely out. She made sure that she was open to anything
that they would ask. So just like that, they dismissed the case.

As soon as they left, she sold all of the food in the
fridge to buy her drugs, leaving me with little to eat. I often
wondered what my dad looked like. Sometimes, I would sit on
the front porch and watch every man that would pass by just to
see if there was any resemblance.

"Claudia, get out here!" My mother yelled from the living room. It took all of my strength to climb out of the bed.

"Yes," I groaned. My mother tapped the ashes from her cigarette into the ashtray and looked at me from top to bottom.

"What is wrong with you?" I shook my head.

"I don't feel too good. My tummy hurts," I said, as I rubbed my stomach.

"There ain't nothing wrong with you," she said, rolling her eyes. "I need you to clean this house, I'm having company tonight." I looked around the two bedroom house, and it was a mess. The excess amount of dishes hid the kitchen sink, and there were clothes all over the living room floor, that flowed into the tiny hallway.

"Mommy, my stomach is really hurting." My mother looked at me with her bloodshot eyes, raising one hand, and slapped me across my face.

"Don't back sass me." I cried and held my hand across my cheek, as I picked up the clothes off of the floor. I, often, hoped that I would die. As I think about it, I was mostly crying because her company always ended up being my molester.

As the years passed, I accepted my life. I accepted that God loved me less than any other little girls that I would see with their families; happy as can be. Or, as though it seemed. I got my first period at the age of twelve. I told my older sister that I had a boyfriend and that we were having sex, just so she could take me to the free clinic to get birth control, but in reality, I didn't want to end up pregnant by no crackhead. I would never forget that day. The nurse walked in the room and told me that she was going to prescribe me some antibiotics, because I had chlamydia. I was confused, at first, to what chlamydia was, but after she explained, I was hysterical. I never told Melissa, because I didn't want to start any drama. I took my medicine and kept an extra stash just in case I needed

it again.

As time went on, I became rebellious, and I was kicked

out of school every other week for fighting. By the time I was

fifteen, I was expelled, so I never returned to school. When I

got home from school the day I was expelled, my mom was

sitting in the living room in the dark.

"Why you sitting in the dark?" I asked, while I tried

flicking on the lights.

"I need you to start working," she stated, avoiding my

question.

"What?" I asked, confused.

"Since you want to be grown and constantly get kicked

out of school, it is time to put you to work. I need help around

here, anyways." She said, while taking a puff of her cigarette.

The judge had recently cut back on her child support since

Melissa and Iyanna were barely home.

"Okay, I will look for a job tomorrow. I know

somebody around here needs a babysitter for their bad kids," I

agreed.

She lit a candle that she had sitting on the black, dusty

end table and walked towards me. "Baby, you start working

tonight." She shoved a two piece swimsuit into my chest and

said, "Get to work."

I stumbled back into the wall. I couldn't believe the

words that flowed out of my mother's mouth.

"Get to work?" I asked, confused.

"You heard me. Get to work. You will be working Rose

Ave. Don't go to no other corner if you want your life," She

instructed, as she blew smoke into my face, causing my eyes to

burn. I fanned the smoke from my face, tossed the clothing on

the floor, and headed towards the door. *I'm not going to take*

this anymore, I told myself. But as I was opening the door, a tall, black man that weighed, I guess, 400 pounds grabbed me

by the neck and tossed me back into the house.

"Meet Fred. Your pimp. You will report to him after

every night of working. You will do what he tell you to do,

because if you don't, he will make sure you suffer," Mother

said, as she squeezed my face.

Tears fell from my eyes, and fear rushed through my

body. I grabbed the two-piece and went into the bathroom to

change. I cried and asked God why he hated me so much. He

never responded... he never did. I walked four blocks down to

Rose Ave, where an old white man stopped by and told me to

get in. Ten minutes later, he dropped me back off on the

corner. I repeated the same thing five more times for the rest of

the night. I felt so empty inside. I was so angry at my mother

and my sisters for never being around. But, mostly, God for

creating me. From that day forward, I just did what I had to do.

As time went on, I became bitter and very cold-hearted. I just didn't care anymore. One night, as I was standing on the street corner, half-naked and scared, I came in contact with some girls that was passing by. Their names were Carrie and Janice, and they had it all. You know, the things that I did not have, like clothes, jewelry, money and the guys. I wanted that... I needed that, so I started hanging out with them, living my life recklessly. They introduced me to a whole new world of drugs and pimps that was making real moves. By the time that I was seventeen, I was selling drugs and dealing with top notch clients that was willing to spend big on a young "tenderoni" like myself. I had to look out for me, because there was no one else that cared about my existence. Nope, not even God!

CHAPTER 2

There was no one in the "game" that was colder than

me. I was making, at least, a thousand dollars a night. Between

selling drugs and myself, I wasn't doing too bad. You had to

get it how you live it. I had been living with my best friend,

Carrie, who was my go to girl; she always had my back. Carrie

was a shy and loving girl. She was very attractive, 5'5, and 150

pounds, with smooth, caramel skin. One night, my mother and

I got into a huge fight, so I had been living at Carrie's house

ever since. That made me really happy, because I didn't have

to deal with my no-count mother anymore.

Through the years, I came to realize that, if you want

something bad enough, you will have to go get it. No one will

ever want it as bad as you. Now, my friend Janice was a

different story. Well, she wasn't really a friend; she was more like a friend of a friend. She was always jealous of me, and I never really understood why. Maybe she felt as though Carrie was more interested in being friends with me than her, or maybe, because I was light-skinned, and she was very dark-skinned. That was something that I would never understand. Beauty was not about your skin color or how your body is shaped. It's about what was within, but, that's how the world thinks. If you are living for the "world", you have to give the world what they want, right?

One night, I had some money stolen from my purse, and there was no one else in the house but Janice and I. I just knew that it was her, but Janice was a big girl, and I did not want to get on her bad side, so I just had to let that go. I was still angry about that money, though, because I owed Sam 500 dollars, and when I didn't have it, I ended up in the hospital for a week, and Carrie was the only one that came to see me.

I guess you're wondering who Sam was. Well, Sam was one of the biggest drug dealers around. He was also my pimp. Sam stood about 6 feet, 4 inches tall, was brown-skinned and had a slender build. He wasn't that attractive in the face, but being a big time drug dealer, women just fell at his feet… including me. No one ever wanted to get on his bad side. I tried explaining that it wasn't my fault and that my money was stolen, but he slapped me around some more for "not taking responsibilities for my own actions." Maybe, I deserved it. At least, that was how I felt at the time. He was like a father that I never had. He took care of me, which was something that my father never did. I guess, I thought that was what having a father felt like. He made sure my money was "managed". He bought me clothes and shoes, and he made sure that I was looking good.

Unfortunately, there was always a price to pay for the finer things in life. Coming from where I came from, that was like a piece of heaven, and he knew it, so he used that to his advantage. Carrie called my mom when I was in the hospital, but she never came, because she was probably off getting high somewhere. She could never help me; she could barely help herself, but I didn't care. I had built up a wall a long time ago just for her.

As I was preparing myself for a night of work and scoping out the best corners to stand on, I came across some guys in a red, 1978 Monte Carlo. The tires had gold rims, just like their teeth, and the driver had on a blue bandana with a scar underneath his left eye. The one on the passenger side was pretty chubby with crooked teeth. As I continued walking, they followed me, shouting out vulgar language.

"Claudia just keep walking; do not make eye contact," I thought to myself, as I walked a little faster, but they would not leave. The driver parked the car as the big chubby dude jumped out at me. I threw off my four-inch heels and ran as fast as I

could! I could barely see the black paved street, as I ran into

the alley, but I kept going. Out of nowhere, came the driver,

with a right hook dead in my eye.

"Where is Sam?! Where is Sam?!" He shouted, as he

punched me.

"I don't know!" I lied.

He continued to kick me with his steel toe boots, as the

other guy searched my purse and my phone. I knew better than

to let them know where Sam was. You might call me crazy, but

I'd rather take a butt whipping from those two guys any day

than to tell on Sam. Besides, I loved Sam; he was there for me,

and he cared for me. At least, that's what I thought. I guess

they got tired of asking me about him, because they started to

walk away.

"Next time, you won't be so lucky! By the way, tell

Sam, Loco is in town, and I miss him!" The driver shouted, as

he slammed his car door and sped off.

My face felt as heavy as a ton of bricks, as blood dripped from my lips. My ribs burned like fire, as I tried to stand to my feet. All I could do was ball myself up in the dark and cold alley and wait until the sunrise. Why was I dealt those cards? Why is my life so hard? Help me Lord! Still..... No answer. As the morning approached, I gained enough strength to walk to the nearest shopping center to call a cab; my phone had died out. It didn't take the cab too long to arrive.

"Are you okay, ma'am?" The cab driver asked, as he looked at me with horror.

"No, I'm fine. Just a rough night, you know," I said, as I stared out the window.

"Okay, where to?" He asked, as he pulled off.

"23rd St., please," I replied, closing my eyes.

About thirty minutes later, I arrived home. "Hold up, I will be right back with your money," I told the taxi driver, as I was opening the car door.

"Okay, make it quick. I don't have all day," The Arab

cab driver yelled, as I walked up the steps. I waved my hand

without looking back. As soon as I walked in the door, Carrie

was waiting for me in the living room.

"Where were you, and what happened?" Carrie

screamed.

I waved her off, as I passed her by. I was just too tired

to explain anything. Janice smacked her lips, as her eyes

followed me down the hall. I grabbed ten bucks off my

nightstand and paid the driver. When I returned back into the

house, Carrie was still standing in the living room, with her

arms folded and her lips tightened, waiting for her answer that I

obviously wasn't about to give. I just wanted to take a bath

and go to sleep. I rushed into the bathroom and jumped straight

into the shower. As the water ran across my body, my cuts

burned like fire, and all I could do was cry. As I was exiting the shower, about fifteen minutes later, I overheard Carrie

telling Janice how horrible I looked.

"Well, maybe she deserved it," Janice stated.

"How could you say such a thing, Janice? She is our

friend, and she needs our help," Carrie replied.

As I continued to dry myself off, and apply peroxide to

my cuts, I could hear Janice yelling at the top of her lungs.

"No! That's your friend. You brought her here, and now

she's bringing all this trouble along with her. Next time, she

won't be so lucky!"

Wow! I thought to myself. *That's the same thing this

Loco character said.* From that day forward, I never looked at

Janice the same. Something just wasn't right with her. I really

didn't trust her now. I just blew it off, laid down in my full-

sized bed, and cried myself to sleep.

A few hours later, Sam was banging on my door.

"Open up, Claudia!" He yelled. His loud knocking startled me out of my sleep. "What happened?" He hollered, as he bombarded his way through the door.

Sam knew something was up, because I never showed up to his place like I normally did after a night of working. I gathered my thoughts and quickly explained to Sam what had happened with the two guys. I just knew that I was about to get my behind beaten, but Sam just stood there with fear all over him. He paced my bedroom floor back and forth, and occasionally, peeked out of the window. I had never seen Sam that scared in my life. I mean, he never admitted that he was scared, but I could tell. His eyes always told on him. Seeing him that scared made me nervous, because he had never showed fear in such a way. Before leaving, he suggested that I stay low for a few days and take some time to rest, but it was never about me; he just didn't want to be found. I agreed and stayed in the house for the rest of the night.

The next morning, around 7 a.m., my baby sis was

ringing my phone. *"Oh God! Does she ever sleep late? I*

thought.

"Well, good morning, sunshine!" I said, sarcastically, as

I answered my phone.

"Humph! Somebody woke up on the wrong side of the

bed I see," Iyanna laughed.

"I'm sorry, girl. It's just that I had a rough few days.

What's up?" I asked, as I placed my hand across my sore ribs

and struggled to sit up.

"Well, I was calling to see if you would like to come to

church with me?" Iyanna responded.

"Not today," I said.

"Whatever!" She said, smacking her lips. You said that

for the last two weeks. What's the excuse today?" I was

becoming a bit annoyed with her questions, because it was too early for that. Even though she was right, I had been avoiding

church for quite some time.

"I just don't feel up to it, little sis. Next time, I'll go. I

promise. Because God is not here; maybe if I go to church, I

will be able to find him," I replied, throwing the covers from

my body.

She went on to say, "God is there; he is everywhere.

You just have to humble yourself to him. You have hardened

your heart so much over the years until the Lord cannot get in.

Baby girl, you have to let things go!" She stated. I rolled my

eyes, placing the phone slightly from my ear.

That was easy for her to say. She had never been

molested, raped, and beaten half to death. She never had to sell

herself so that mother could go get high. How could she have

possibly known how I felt? Maybe, God was hiding himself

from a no-count like me.

"Next time, Iyanna," I promised. "By the way, how is Melissa doing?" I asked, changing the subject.

"She is fine. You know she finally got that promotion on her job," Iyanna said, excitingly.

Melissa had been working with the CIA for over seven years now. I wasn't a bit surprised, though, because she was always so smart. I was always jealous of her. Not because she looked better than me or had a legit job, but because she had family.

"Good for her!" I said, as I stood in front of the mirror looking over my scarred lips. The thought of those two guys made my stomach hurt.

"Okay, Claudia, I have to go, but I will hold you to your word. Talk to you soon," Iyanna said. I agreed before hanging up.

Shortly after hanging up with baby sis, I received an anonymous phone call.

"Hello?" I asked.

"How have you been, Claudia?" I paused, as I heard a
deep male's voice.

"Umm, who is this?" I asked, placing one hand on my
hip.

"This is Melvin. Did you forget my voice that fast?" He
said, with aggravation in his voice.

"Hey, Mel! Well, it has been a couple of years since we
last spoke," I responded.

"It sure has. Time moves so fast. So, tell me, how have
you been? Have you been staying out of trouble?" He probed.

"Umm...I been surviving, and you?" I replied, as I
worked my way into the bathroom.

"I been really great! God has been blessing me as I
bless him. The reason why I'm calling is because I will be in
town next month for a minister's seminar, and I wanted to
catch up."

Melvin and I grew up on the same street. When he was only fifteen, his mother passed away, so after that, he moved to Illinois with his dad. Melvin was now an ordained minister up in Illinois. He was very handsome and was more like a pretty boy. He was someone that I would admire from afar but never wanted to date.

"Yes, I would love to catch up, as long as you don't drill the Lord down my throat," I joked between brushing my teeth.

Mel chuckled a little, and said, "That's a promise. I will contact you in a few weeks. Take care."

After hanging up with Melvin, I went back into my room, laid across my bed, and reminisced about the good 'ole days. When I would go over to Melvin's house to hangout, his mother was always so pleasant. Sometimes, I would pretend like she was my mother, and I was so sad when she passed away. A lot had changed since then. Melvin always did show up when things were pretty chaotic in my life. He always had a

way of putting a little joy in my day, but that didn't last too

long, because the following days were filled with a whole

bunch of drama! My 21st birthday was approaching, and it was

time for me to start planning my huge house party. Even

though my lifestyle had me feeling like I had been 21 for years

now, surviving another year was always something to celebrate.

"So, Carrie, are you going to help me plan this party, or

what?" I asked, as I walked into Carrie's room. Carrie never

liked planning anything; she was the type to just go with the

flow.

"Girl, when were you planning on starting since your

birthday is three weeks from now?" She asked, with a frown

on her face.

"Okay, girl, I know party planning is not your thing, but

it's my 21st, and I want to make it special. I was thinking that, maybe, we can start today," I said, with a giant smile on my face. Carrie could never resist my perfect teeth. That was one thing that I did have that was perfect; my smile.

"I guess I will help since it's so special to you," Carrie said, rolling her eyes.

"Yay! This party will be everything!" I screamed, as I danced and snapped my fingers. As I took a moment from celebrating to look over at Carrie, I could tell that something was bothering her, because she was slumped over her twin-sized bed.

"What's the matter?" I asked, worried, as I sat next to her. All she could do was hold her hands in her face and cry.

"I'm pregnant!" I had never mentioned this, but Carrie was "In Love" with this married man from across town. He started off as one of her clients, but she ended up falling for him. He was the type that thought he was so much better than our "type." I've always told Carrie that he was no good and that she could do better.

"So, Carrie, does he know about the baby?" I asked, as I handed her a tissue.

"He does, and he said it's not by him and that I'm just a tramp on the streets that's trying to take everything that he has," she continued to cry.

"Girl, I told you from the beginning that this was going to end up ugly. So, what are you going to do?" I questioned.

"I will keep it," Carrie responded. "And I don't care what he has to say about it. Did he ask his wife to kill their three kids when she got pregnant? No! There is no difference other than the fact that I'm not her. It's still his flesh and blood." She walked over to her mirror and rubbed on her stomach. "I'm just so confused." Carrie said, as tears fell from her eyes. I walked over to comfort her.

"Well, girl, you know I have your back all the way. No matter what you want to do, I am here." Holding her in my arms, I could feel so much hurt, but as the old saying goes, "if you knew better, you would do better." I wiped Carrie's tears and pulled her by her arm. "Come on, girl. Let's start this party planning. There is no need to sit and mope around on something that we do not have any control over."

She wiped her eyes and said, "I guess you're right. It has been a long day."

I think I have reached my max with the drama today. I thought to myself, as I grabbed my car keys, but little did I know that the drama in my life did not have a max. Later on that night, as Carrie and I was shopping, we met up with one of Sam's women, Jackie. I looked over to my right only to see that Jackie was watching me, as she was standing in the checkout line next to me.

"Uh, do you have a problem, Jackie?" I asked.

If she would have stared at me any harder, her eyes would have popped out of her head. Jackie was always dressed to "impress". Everywhere she went, she turned heads. She had her black, clingy dress on, with her six-inch heels. She always made sure that her extensions hung right below her waist. Her famous words were, *"it doesn't matter where you are; you always have to be ready to make that money."*

"Yes, I do, as a matter of fact," she said, walking towards me pointing her finger in the air. "What do you think you're too good to work now?" Jackie asked, staring at me up and down. "Miss Goodie, goodie." Her ugly friend cosigned. Jackie was always jealous of me, because Sam gave me more attention than her.

"Girl, what are you talking about?" I asked, while putting up my guards, just in case, she tried something. "You know what? It does not matter." I said, waving her off.

The old white lady standing in front of me turned to look at me making the scene more awkward than it already was.

"No, it does matter!" She yelled, while rolling her neck.

Oh, God! Why is she trying me in this store in front of these people? I thought to myself.

She continued her ranting. "When I have to take your place and work a double because the little princess can't work!"

I didn't have time for that tonight. I placed my few items aside and attempted to walk out of the store, but as I was walking away, I felt a big knock on the back of my head. I grabbed the back of my head and turned to notice an apple on the ground. The whole room turned red. I WAS FURIOUS!

"I know this rat did not just throw an apple at my darn head!" You must have lost your mind!" I screamed, as I ran towards her, knocking her down to the ground.

"Ma'am, get off of her! And, get out of this store this instance!" A long, bearded man yelled from behind the service desk. "And, I'm calling the cops!" He shouted, with the receiver in his hand.

"Come on, girl," Carrie said, while pulling me apart from Jackie.

"This isn't over! I will see you!" Jackie screamed. I nodded my head in agreement. If it wasn't one thing, it surely was another.

CHAPTER 3

The next morning, I was awakened to the sound of
gunshots.

Boom! Boom! Boom!

"God!" I yelled. "I'm so tired of waking up to these
fools always trying to kill someone in these streets!"

Who needed an alarm clock when you had these fools,
faithfully, waking you up every day, at the same time with their
nonsense? I pulled the covers over my head and said my
morning prayer, hoping that it would be a better day than
yesterday. As I rolled over to look at my phone, I noticed that I
had twenty-three missed calls. Twenty from Sam alone.

I gave out a loud sigh, "What in the world does he want
now!" I was growing so sick of Sam and his mess. Before I
could return his phone call, my phone was ringing.

"Hello!" I yelled, as I sat up against my headboard.

"Where the hell have you been?! I've been calling you all night!" Sam yelled.

"I was sleeping, and my ringer was off. I'm up now. What is the matter?" I replied.

"I'm coming over!" He said, as he hung up the phone.

Lord, help me, because I don't know what will happen when he gets here. I, immediately, jumped out of my bed and got dressed. I had to be prepared for anything. I greased my face up in Vaseline and tied my curls back. Then, I made sure to put on my running shoes. About fifteen minutes later, Sam arrived. As soon as I opened the door, Sam was all in my face yelling!

"What happened to you last night? Did you forget about the deal that we set up a couple of weeks ago?" He said, pointing back and forth between him and I. "You cost me a lot of money! Instead of going around attacking people, you should have been making my money." Sam's breath made me dizzy. It smelled like old wine and skunk. I took a step back to minimize the funk that was consuming my thoughts.

"Tell your women to stay in their own lane, and they wouldn't get their behind whooped. And, anyways, I was tired, and I had a lot on my mind; I just forgot!" I explained, with an attitude, as I walked to the kitchen. I was so sick of Sam telling me what to do. I just wished that, that Loco guy would get rid of him already. Pointing and shouting, Sam followed me into the kitchen.

"Well, you will have to pay me for my loss," he commanded.

"And, what's that?" I asked.

"Twelve hundred!" He shouted. I pretended to look around for his mind that he had obviously lost.

"I do not have that type of money, anymore! You told me to lay low, did you forget?" I asked.

"Well, I need my money!" Sam demanded. "So it's time to get back to work!" He slammed his fist down on the cabinet, with his teeth clenched together.

"Go get it yourself," I mumbled.

"What did you say?" Sam asked, holding his finger behind his ear, as though to hear me better.

"You heard me," I answered, not believing the words that were coming from my mouth. Sam face folded, as he raised his hand to slap me, but he never got a chance, because right when he was about to, the police were knocking at the door.

I had never been so happy to see the police in my life. Even though they may be here for me for whooping Jackie's behind yesterday, I didn't care. I opened the door, and there were two cops standing on the porch. One black and the other white.

"How may I help you officers?" I asked, timidly.

"Yes, we're looking for Samuel Johnson. Would you happen to know of his whereabouts?" The officer asked, as he peeked through my door.

The look on Sam's face was the picture of death. Sam's eyes widened so big, and his breathing became swift. He tried running out the back door, but to his surprise, there was a cop waiting for him on the other side. It seemed as though his luck had finally ran out.

"I will kill you, Claudia, for setting me up!" He yelled, with evil in his eyes, as the cops positioned him into the car. Sam was just like a child, as he yelled and kicked at the windows. He was yelling out words that I couldn't make out. I just stood there in the door way, frozen with disbelief, as the police pulled away with my pimp/lover. I wanted to let him know that it wasn't me that set him up, but my words never came out. That scenery brought me back to a place where I'd rather not go.

****

"Everybody put your hands up!" The policer officer shouted, as they bombarded their way through the house. There was dope and prostitutes everywhere. My mom had been M.I.A. for the last few days, and she had left Fred in charge of the house while she was gone.

"Officer, please, we didn't do anything wrong," Fred begged, as he laid on the floor with his hands in the air.

"Shut your mouth!" The officer shouted, as he pointed his gun in Fred's face.

"Who is the owner of this house?" The officer asked, as he looked around the drug-infested house. I raised my hand in fear.

"Me, officer." I said, between swallows. *"Well, I live here with my mother. She pays the rent here."* The officer walked up to me.

"What's your name?" He said, as he looked at me from top to bottom. I didn't know if he was admiring my body or if he felt sorry for me. I could never tell the difference.

"My name is Claudia James, and I'm only sixteen years old," I responded, timidly.

Not responding, he yelled, *"Alright, round them up, and see if you can get in touch with this young lady's mother,"* he said, placing his sunglasses over his eyes.

They took Fred and the rest of the gang to prison. I stayed in a group home until they contacted my mother a month later. She denied knowing anything about drugs or the fact that Fred was her pimp. Then, she testified against him in court, which gave her only three months in jail. She and I were back together in no time, and I was very disappointed. We *ended up in a one bedroom apartment, and I was back working*

the blocks. That was one of the saddest days of my life.

****

A few days later, Carrie and I was riding around in her

beat up 1997 Toyota Camry, having girl talk.

"Claudia, I had a dream about you the other night,"

Carrie said.

"Oh! Really? What about?" I asked, as I looked over at

her, strangely, raising one eyebrow.

"You was in an all-white dress, standing in a forest,

dancing and singing. It was like you had pure joy," she said.

Ha! That's a dream alright. A dream I wish would

come true, I thought to myself.

"I have really been thinking about giving my life to

Christ," Carrie said, as she pulled into a vacant parking lot that

was once surrounded by stores. Every time Carrie was serious

about something, she made sure that she had my undivided

attention. "I mean, I have nothing to lose. My life is just a

complete mess. It feels as though I am going straight to hell. At

times, I feel like I am in hell. So, what am I waiting for? My

parents disowned me ever since I moved out. I just don't know

where else to turn."

The way Carrie was feeling was how I felt all of the

time. I just learned to push my feelings aside. Growing up the

way I did, it was best not to have feelings at all. "That makes a

lot of sense," I said, as I took one of my ultra slim cigarettes

from my purse and lit it. "I mean, I thought about it many of

times, but it was like no matter what I did, trouble always

seemed to find me. It was like... I was cursed!" I said, as I flicked my ashes out of the window and blew my smoke in the

opposite direction of Carrie.

I always smoked when things were bothering me, it

helped keep me sane. A bad habit that I wished to get rid of.

"Girl, if you pray hard enough, those chains will be broken.

Thank God for my praying grandmother," Carrie said, as she

stared out of the window.

Humph, as for my grandmother, she has been in prison

since my mother was fifteen years old. She was sentenced to

life without parole for killing two police officers. Carrie

interrupted my thoughts.

"I know! Let's-go-to-church!" She said, while clapping

in-between her words. I humped my shoulders.

"I don't know girl." I tossed my cigarette bud out the

window.

"Come on, Claudia! Besides, we both need the Lord in

our lives and tomorrow isn't promised. I most definitely do not want to spend my eternity in hell." Carrie cranked up her car

and pulled out of the parking lot. "Please just do it for me," she

begged.

"Okay, for you, I will go, but let's plan this party. We

only have two weeks left to do it.

"Ugh!" Carrie frowned. We laughed, as we drove back

home.

Two weeks had finally passed, and it was my birthday.

It was time to party!

"Happy Birthday, Chick!" Carrie screamed.

"Thanks, hunni bunny. I am so excited about tonight.

We will have so much fun!" I said, as I twirled pass Carrie.

"Did you call your family and invite them?" Carrie

asked, as she put some finishing touches on the decorations in

the living area.

"Oh no, girl. They wouldn't be caught dead around the folks we hang with, but I did receive a phone call from my sisters," I mentioned.

"What about your mother?" Carrie probed.

"No, I probably wouldn't have answered anyways," I lied.

I was a little disappointed that she didn't call, but that was nothing new, and I was not going to let that ruin my day. Once Carrie was finished with the decorations, I took a step back in admiration. I didn't have to say a word; she knew I loved it.

She patted me on my back, and said, "You welcome."

I gave out a light chuckle and went and prepared myself for a night of fun. As the night approached, the house became so packed. My decorations were on point; Carrie had really outdone herself. My theme colors were pink and green, which were always my two favorite colors. Instead of a red carpet runway, my runway was pink, and I had the most beautiful

birthday cake that any girl could have asked for! Red velvet...

my favorite. I was so happy, because growing up, I never really

had a birthday cake, besides the one that Melissa tried to make

me when we were kids.

****

"Happy birthday." Melissa whispered, as she kissed me

on my cheek.

I turned over on my side and gave a huge smile. It was

a cold January 21st, and it was my tenth birthday.

"Thank you," I said, as I sat up and gave her a hug.

"I have something for you," Melissa said, placing one

finger across her lips and closing the room door. She walked

towards the closet and took out a box that was wrapped in pink and green wrapping paper. My eyes must have lit up with joy, because Melissa gave out a giggle.

"Go ahead. Open it, silly," she said, as she handed me the box. I quickly tore off the wrapping and opened the box.

"Wow!" I said, as I admired the bracelet inside that said "world's greatest little sister." I had never received any type of gift before. I knew that it was Melissa's dad that cared enough to buy me something. "Thank you so much, Melissa," I cried.

I hadn't cried tears of joy in so long, if ever. My joy was, immediately, crushed when the bedroom door swung open. It was my mother.

"What in the hell do we have here?" She jerked my bracelet right out of my hand.

"Give it here, mommy. Melissa gave me that," I begged.

"Tell that no good daddy of yours not to be sending my daughter anything. All he has to do is send me my check every month!" She yelled, while pointing her finger in Melissa's face.

"But, it's Claudia's birthday," Melissa said, as she grabbed me around my waist.

"We don't celebrate birthdays around here. Celebrate for what? Another year in this hell hole of a world? That's not anything to celebrate," Mother said, slurring her words. It was only 9 a.m., and she was drunk already.

"I hate you!" I screamed, as I dashed onto my bed and cried my eyes out. Melissa stood there in tears.

"I need some more liquor. I think I know somebody that will buy this from me," Mother said, as she dangled the bracelet in the air. She laughed and walked out the door.

"I'm sorry, sissy," Melissa said, as she sat down beside the bed. My heart was too hurt to say another word. As soon as my mother left the house, Melissa jumped up.

*"Come on. Let's make you a cake." I looked at Melissa,
as though she was crazy.*

*"Momma said we can't," I said, as I sat up and placed
my feet on the cold floor.*

*"Come on. We will make a small one." Melissa
grabbed my hand and pulled me into the kitchen. She grabbed
the flour, sugar, eggs, and the milk. She rolled all the
ingredients into one. Then, she poured it into a small pan and
set the oven. In no time, my birthday cake was complete. It was
the worst tasting cake that I had ever eaten, but it was the best
birthday ever, because of Melissa. The only thing that was
missing was Iyanna, because she was visiting with her dad. We
were able to hide the evidence before my mother could return.
Those were the little moments of God saying, "I love you, and I
hadn't forgotten about you."*

****

"Happy Birthday!" Everyone shouted.

"Thank you, my beautiful people. Let's show this block how to really party, and if the cops comes knocking, we ain't stopping!" I shouted.

Everyone yelled in agreement and continued dancing. I had one of the hottest DJ's in the town. Everything was going as planned and was getting along. I had on the cutest pink jumpsuit that fit my small physique just right, and I strutted my stuff in my bad black red bottom pumps. I was all that, and Sam was in jail. I was feeling so good. I felt free for the very first time.

"Hey girl. Do you need anything from the store? We ran out of chips and dip," Carrie asked, as she danced in circles around me.

"No!" I shouted, because the music was so loud.

"Okay, girl. I will be right back. Love you!" Carrie said, as she leaned in to give me a hug.

"Love you, too, Chick," I said, as I did the cabbage patch; a dance that I had always loved doing. I looked back at Carrie to thank her again for an outstanding job on my party. I was so grateful.

As I was walking back towards the kitchen, I heard a loud bang that, immediately, made me freeze, because I knew, in my heart, that Carrie was hurt. Dropping everything, I took off running through the crowd as fast as I could. My heart was racing, as I opened the front door. My body became fragile, as I saw Carrie lying there on the cold ground, and my heart stopped.

"What happened?!" Someone yelled from behind me. I took a deep breath and dropped down to my knees, as I tried to wake her up.

Kathleen D.
Richardson

056

"She's been shot!" I cried.

"Carrie, get up! Carrie, get up!" I yelled, with tears rolling down my face. Blood was everywhere; it had stained her beautiful pink dress. I couldn't believe what I was seeing, right before my eyes. "Call 9-1-1! Please… somebody call 9-1-1!" I cried out, as I rocked her in my arms, but it was too late. She was already gone.

I didn't say a word for, at least, five hours. My body felt so numb. *How could this happen? How could this be? This is my fault. I wanted this stupid party. If I didn't have this party, she would still be alive!* I was so confused, and I just wanted to die. After everyone was gone, I tried to sleep, but I just couldn't. I just tossed and turned, thinking, wondering, and trying to find a solution where there wasn't one. I popped pills after pills, but nothing could heal the hurt and emptiness that I was feeling. That was an eye-opener, for sure. I tried calling Janice, but she wasn't answering her phone. I didn't want to call my sisters. I didn't feel like the lectures tonight. I was

alone with just me and my thoughts.

The next day, the police stopped by to gather a

statement from me. All I could think about was Sam and what

he said that day the cops took him away. *That bullet was meant*

for me. I really didn't have any hope in the police, because they

were so tired of us killing one another until they didn't really

care anymore. Sometimes, I didn't blame them for not caring.

"Okay, I've written down everything that you told me,

and I will be in touch very soon," The officer said.

All I could do was nod my head. All I was thinking

about was paying Sam a visit. Later that evening, my sister,

Melissa, came by the house to check on me. That was a

surprise, because even though she grew up in the hood, she

never came to the hood. When she left, she left. She pulled up

in her white BMW, which her dad bought for her when she

graduated from college. Melissa's dad was an Italian, top-notch, cardiologist surgeon. He wanted a prostitute for the night and ended up with a daughter for the rest of his life. I gave him props, because he always took care of his child, no matter how she was conceived.

"How are you doing?" Melissa asked, as she leaned in to hug me.

"Horrible!" I said, with tears in my eyes. I didn't sleep at all last night."

"Well, that is to be expected. Have you decided where you will be living?" She asked, as she bent down to sit next to me.

"Here. Why would you ask that? Do you expect me to leave my home?" I questioned, giving her attitude.

"Look, before you jump up my behind, all I'm saying is whoever shot her may decide to come back." Melissa stated, concerned.

Why was she concerned? She wasn't willing to take me into her fancy home with her stuck-up husband and his kid. Ever since Melissa got with Gary, our relationship had changed.

"I don't know, and I really don't care. Maybe they can finish what they started, because I know that bullet was meant for me. From God, himself," I said, as I stood and paced the porch back and forth and watched every car that passed by.

"Don't say that!" She yelled.

"How do you know that? Wasn't Carrie pregnant by a married man?" Melissa questioned, while smacking her hand in rage on the cemented steps.

"The police already investigated, and he proved he was out of town. He was out of town with his wife and his in-laws," I responded. "I know it was Sam. I just know it," I mumbled, as I lit my cigarette.

Melissa walked up to me and slapped my cigarette out

of my hand. I didn't bother to fuss with her about my cigarette,

because I would have never won.

"Focus, Claudia! Who is Sam, and what do you know?"

Melissa asked, grabbing me around my shoulders. Melissa was

transforming into "C.I.A. Melissa" real quick.

"Never mind, I'm okay. I will be okay. And, will you

calm down? You are not at work," I said, brushing her off.

"I sure hope so," she said, ungrasping my shoulders.

"You know, Mother has really been worried about you. I think

that she will finally get the help that she needs." Melissa

believed. If she only knew what I knew about her dear mother,

she wouldn't be so hopeful for her.

"Can we not talk about that lady? I am upset enough as

it is," I demanded.

Melissa walked up to me, and said, "I don't know what

it is that you can't forgive her for, but we endured the same drunken/druggy mother that you had to endure. If we were able to forgive her, so can you. You will have to face her one day; If not for her, for you." I flipped through my phone, as I ignored her comment. "Well, if you need anything, just let me know," she said, as she kissed me upon my cheek.

"I will. Thanks, sissy," I said, with no eye contact. Melissa jumped in her car and drove off. I smoked about ten cigarettes before returning into the house for the remainder of the day. I turned my phone off and locked my bedroom door, because I did not want to be disturbed.

The next morning, I was up pretty early. It was time to pay Sam a visit. I hopped out of the shower and realized that I was out of deodorant. I wasn't about to ask Janice for hers, so I had to go into Carrie's room. I grabbed the door knob and took a deep breath before turning and pushing it open. Her scent filled my nostrils, as I entered into her room. My heart tensed, as the tears started to flow. I, quickly, walked towards her dresser, where she had all of her accessories lined up. I giggled to myself, as I remembered how much of a clean freak she was.

"Carrie, you are so O.C.D.," I said, reaching for the deodorant. I stood there for a moment, as I placed her stuff back into place. "I will never forget you," I mumbled, as I took one last look and closed the door.

I, quickly, grabbed my car keys and hit the road. On my way there, I listened to Tupac's, "Me Against the World." Tupac always seemed to pump me up for that type of occasion. After driving for four hours, I finally arrived. Sam eyes flamed with fire, as I approached him.

"What are you doing here? You have some nerves coming here after what you've done to me," he assumed, balling up his fist, as though he was about to do something.

"Whatever. Think what you want!" I said, waving my hands in the air. *I was not trying to hear what Sam had to say. I came here for answers, and I was planning on burying Sam in jail.* "But, do you want to explain why you sent your friends to shoot up my house?" I asked. My blood was boiling, as I waited for his answer.

"I don't know what you're talking about. You better get away from here accusing me of something that I did not do. Besides, you have many enemies of your own," Sam said, angrily under his breath, trying not to draw attention our way.

"Stop screwing with me, Sammie! I know it was you. And, it's because of you that Carrie is dead!" I screamed.

"Say what? Carrie is dead?" Sam voice, squeaked.

Why is he so hurt? I thought.

"You heard me," I responded.

"Well, I didn't have anything to do with that. Besides, I really cared for Carrie," Sam said, clearing his throat.

"Oh really? Did you?" I asked, puzzled.

Sam took a deep breath and folded his hands on the hard steel table in front of him. He, then, put his head down like a scared little kid. "I might as well tell you. Carrie and I

were seeing each other." I sat there in disbelief for a moment

and studied Sam's face.

"What? Liar!" I shouted. Even though, in my heart, I

knew that he wasn't lying. I was in deep denial. At that point,

the guards had enough of my outbursts.

"Ma'am, you will have to leave!" One of the officer's

instructed.

"Sam, you are a liar. Carrie would have never betrayed

me like this! How could you say such a thing?" I continued

yelling. Sam just sat there with his head in his hands.

"Ma'am, let's go!" The guard snapped his fingers at me,

and they grabbed me by my arms and dragged me out.

CHAPTER 4

It was taking me some time to process what Sam had just revealed to me. I really didn't feel like involving Janice in my business, but I had some questions that needed some answers. As I was approaching Janice, I could tell that she was going to have an attitude, but I didn't care.

"Janice, can I ask you something?" I asked, as I stood in the doorway of the bathroom where Janice was curling her hair.

"What?" Janice responded, as she smacked her lips. I rolled my eyes, while ignoring her attitude.

"Did Carrie ever mention anything about her and Sam messing around?" I asked, nonchalantly, as I tried to hold myself together. Janice stopped combing through her hair to focus her attention towards me.

"Who told you that?" Janice had a puzzled look on her face.

"Sam," I answered.

"Well, yes," she replied.

"What do you mean, well yes?" I asked, eagerly.

"Well yes, they were involved for like six months," Janice replied, with an evil grin on her face.

"So, the baby?" I asked, as my heart pounded out of my chest.

"I don't know about that, because she was still messing with that other guy, so your guess is just as good as mine. Anyways, that does not matter, because Carrie had an abortion like a week before she died," Janice said, as she placed her ear buds in her ears and walked away.

"What?!" I tried yelling out to Janice, as she made her way to her room.

I banged on her door, yelling for her to open up and talk to me, but she just ignored me like she always did. *This could not be true!* My heart dropped to the floor. *Who was she? Did I even know her at all? I looked up to her. How could she betray me like this?* My mind was spinning out of control, as the tears raced down my face. I felt like there was no one that I could ever trust again. I didn't care, and my heart turned so cold. I just wanted to be alone. Her betrayal brought back so many memories that I only hoped to forget. I closed myself up in my room for the rest of the day and cried myself to sleep.

****

"I'm sure glad we are friends, Ashley," I said, as I sat across from the most popular girl in the eighth grade. Ashley gave me a well-lit smile.

"Me, too. Would you like to come over after school?"

Her words made my heart fill up with joy. I had never had a

friend like her before. I was always over-looked, because of the

shoes on my feet and the clothes on my back. My hair was

always nappy, and I smelled badly from time-to-time, from the

lack of deodorant at home. Ashely was the only one in class

that would talk to me. Mainly, about my answers on my test,

but she still talked to me.

"I sure would love to come over," I responded,

cheerfully.

I didn't bother going home after school. I was too

excited to hang out with Ashley. She had two older brothers

whose names were Mike and Jimmy. Mike was the popular

football player, while Jimmy was mentally impaired. As we

approached her house, I noticed that Ashley's mother wasn't

home.

*"Does your mother work?" I asked, as I played through
my nappy curls. Even though my mother allowed strange men
to violate me, she always told me not to visit anyone while their
parents wasn't home.*

*"Yes, but she will be home shortly," she reassured. We
walked to the back door where Jimmy was sitting on the steps.*

*"Hey, Jimmy. This is Claudia, and she came to play
with you," she said, as she played through Jimmy's shaggy
sandy brown hair. I laughed it off, not thinking anything of it.
Jimmy extended his hand towards me without making any eye
contact. I made a face at Ashley, hoping she would tell her
brother that she was only joking, but she didn't.*

*"Go ahead. Touch him. You do allow men to touch you
like your slutty mother, right?" Ashley asked, as she laughed
and stomped her feet in amusement. My stomach twisted into
knots.*

"What is this? I thought we were going to hang out?" I

asked, with tears in my eyes.

"I would never be caught dead with someone like you.

If you thought that, then you're just as dumb as Jimmy," she

responded, while pointing at Jimmy. My heart began to

tremble at the very thought of her words. I felt so angry and so

betrayed. My mind became blank, as I rushed towards her,

latching onto her neck. Jimmy stood up and grabbed me by my

hair and dragged me into the house. I screamed and I kicked,

as I fought to free myself from the 200 pound, 6 feet, white

giant, but he overpowered me and knocked me out.

The next thing I knew, I was laid out on an old

basement floor, naked and beaten with Jimmy launched over

me. I was being raped. I began to cry and scream for my life.

Jimmy placed his hands over my mouth causing me to beg for

air. I didn't want to die, so I shut up and let it happen. Mike

and Jimmy threatened to kill and expose me, if I ever told anyone. I grabbed my Ked's and ran two miles home without

stopping. I cried out to God as I ran home, hoping that he

would make me disappear. I vowed to never trust a friend

again.

****

Ring! Ring!

My phone rung, waking me out of my peaceful sleep. I

wiped my eyes and looked over at my clock. It was 10 p.m.,

and I was going to ignore it, but I noticed that it was Melvin, so

I decided to pick up.

"Hello," I answered, as I strolled down the dark hall to

the bathroom.

"Hey, Claudia. How are you? Sorry to call so late, but I

will be in town in the morning, and I was hoping that you were available?" It was good to hear Melvin's voice, and it was just

what I needed.

"Oh, God. I forgot you was coming into town. So much

has been going on," I said, before flushing the toilet.

"How about we catch some lunch tomorrow and talk

about it?" Melvin insisted.

"Okay, we can do that," I said, with hesitance in my

voice, because I was looking and feeling a mess. I knew that I

could really use some positive company, though. "How does 11

o'clock sound to you, Melvin?" I suggested, as I looked in the

mirror with disgust.

Of all days, a pimple had to show up right in the middle

of my forehead.

He, anxiously, responded, "Sounds good to me. See you

tomorrow." I hung up the phone and snuggled my way back

into my sheets.

The following day, Melvin and I met up at this cozy bistro downtown. When I arrived, Melvin was already there waiting on me.

"Good morning, I'm meeting up with someone," I said to the petite waitress.

"Name?" She asked, as she looked down at a sheet of paper on the podium.

"Melvin Woodman," I responded.

"Oh yes! This way please." She directed me to a small table in the corner by the window.

"Hey, Ms. Claudia!" Melvin said, with excitement, as he stood up to greet me.

"Well, hey yourself! You surely do look well," I responded, as I admired his physique. Melvin was really looking good these days. He had on a white V-neck tee and a pair of dark blue 501 Levi's. The aroma of Tom Ford filled the air as he leaned in to kiss me on my cheek.

"It has been a long time. You haven't changed a bit," Melvin said, as he looked at me from top to bottom. Little did he know that a lot had changed over the years. He didn't know that I was a complete mess.

"Sit and tell me what's been going on with you over these years. Do you have any kids? Are you married?" He asked, as he pulled out the wooden padded chair from the table.

"No kids, and no one special. How about you?" I replied, as I sat down.

"Unfortunately, God has not sent my queen, yet, and I have been celibate for over two years now," he replied, as he took his seat.

"Oh! Wow, good for you. You have always been a good man. You know? One of the honest ones. You're surely not like any of the fools that I have dealt with in my days," I said, shaking my head.

Mel chuckled. "Well, I don't know about all of that. Trust me, I have my flaws."

Humph, where they at, because I don't see them. I thought to myself. *He was like Jesus compared to these no good drug dealers that I dealt with, but they did say you have to watch them "church folks."* My thoughts were interrupted by the petite waitress.

"Hello! My name is Karen. I will be serving you guys today. Can I get you all anything to drink?" The petite waitress asked, as she placed a basket of rolls on the table.

"Yes, I will have a raspberry tea." I ordered.

"For you, sir?" The waitress asked Melvin.

"A water will be fine for now," Melvin responded.

"Okay, sounds good. I will get that to you right away," the waitress said, as she made a quick note on her notepad. We nodded our heads "okay", as she walked off.

"God, it has been so long Melvin! I can't believe how much you've changed. You use to be a knucklehead," I said, laughing.

Melvin nodded his head in agreement. "You are right about that!" We continued to laugh.

About five minutes later, the waitress was back with our drinks.

"Are you all ready to order?" She asked, placing our drinks on the table.

"Can you give us another ten minutes?" Melvin suggested.

"No problem. Once again, my name is Karen. Just let me know when you are ready," she said.

"Okay, thanks!" Melvin and I responded at once. She smiled and went to assist the table next to us.

"So, how long will you be in town for?" I asked, as I sipped on my raspberry tea, which was one of my all-time favorites.

"I will be out here for a couple of weeks. I have some things that I need to catch up on," Melvin said, with a smile on his face and a twinkle in his eyes.

I know Melvin was not calling himself flirting with me. I thought to myself. Just when I was about to excuse myself from the table to use the restroom, Loco and "Chubby" popped up at our table.

Oh my God! What do these fools want? I thought to myself, as my heart began to race.

"Hey, my sweet lady. Long time, no see. Loco said has he pulled up a chair to the table. Chubby gave a nod, as he stood by the small window overshadowing the sun. "Did you get a chance to tell Sam that I was looking for him? I thought he would have known after I sent him that friendly reminder,"

Loco said, as he buttered one of the rolls on the table.

"What type of reminder?" I asked, as I jerked the roll

from his hand. "Besides, he is in jail. Is that what you are

talking about?" Loco looked at me with a blank stare.

"How was your party the other night? I heard it really

ended with a bang," he said, sarcastically. My heart froze.

Flashbacks of that night came rushing to me all at once.

"How do you know I had a party?" I asked confused.

Not responding, Loco turned his attention towards Melvin.

"So who is your friend?" Loco pointed his finger

towards Melvin.

"I am Melvin, who are you?" Melvin responded, with

an attitude. Now, Melvin had given his life to Christ, but don't

let that fool you. He had it in him. He hadn't always been

saved. Loco turned towards "Chubby", and they begin to laugh,

mocking Melvin.

"Olé' boy has an attitude," Chubby teased.

"Calm down, Potna! I'm a really good friend of Claudia's, and she owes me some money. I'm just trying to resolve this matter," Loco said, as he cracked his knuckles.

"Wait a minute! First of all, I don't know you. Secondly, I don't owe you anything!" I yelled, slamming my hand on the wooden table. Loco got up from the table to sit closer to where I was, with a blackness in his eyes.

"Whatever Sam owes me, you owe me," he stated in a calm, but creepy, voice.

I could feel something poking me in my ribs. I looked down, and there it was... a gun! "Oh My God! I don't have anything to do with this," I cried.

Melvin stood up. "Get away from her!" Melvin yelled, but before he could come around to where I was, "Chubby" put a gun to his back.

"Sit your tall, lanky behind down, before I shoot you down, pretty boy!" He threatened.

"Melvin, please, just sit down!" I cried. This was starting to feel like Déjà vu.

****

"Who are these guys that Janice set us up with?" I asked, as I brushed through my tight curls.

"Just some guys her homeboy, John, knows," Carrie responded. We were preparing ourselves for a night of working. Two Italian guys were interested in three young black females for the night, and we fit that criteria, but something just didn't feel right about that set up. I mean, Janice's encounters in the past were legit, but something just wasn't sitting right in my gut with that one.

"Hurry up, yawl. We will be late! A lot of money is on the line here!" Janice yelled from the living room. I slipped on my petite leather skirt, my yellow tube top, and my four-inch heels. I grabbed my mace, and we were out the door.

Twenty minutes later, we were pulling up to a millionaire's mansion. We hadn't had this type of job in a long time. The last one that we did have, didn't go over so well. Let's just say that some things some guys were into were pretty weird and disgusting. If I could've traded my brain for a new one, I would, just to wipe out the memories.

"I don't know about this Janice. I mean, we are in the middle of nowhere. I'm still trying to understand why we couldn't bring our phones?" I stated, as I looked around the dark yard that was surrounded by huge oak trees.

"Look, Claudia! You're here now, so chill out!" Janice turned and yelled, violently, in my face.

"Calm down Janice, dang! It will be okay, girl. We got

this in the bag," Carrie said, winking her eye at me, as she

applied her favorite plum lip gloss on.

"I guess you're right," I said, rolling my eyes at Janice.

We walked up to the house and rang the doorbell. Two Italian

guys greeted us at the door.

"Come on in, and take a sit in the dining area." One of

the Italian guys motioned for us down the large foyer. There

were crystals everywhere. The floors were marble, and the

ceilings were, easily, 20 feet high.

What I wouldn't do to marry a guy with this type of

luxury. Not even God has this type of money. I said to myself,

as I sat on the leather chair.

"So, tell me, ladies, what is it that we are doing on this

beautiful night, Aye?"

The tall, dark, and handsome Italian asked in a heavy

accent. Janice got up and slowly walked up to him and began to dance, while Carrie and I sipped on our drinks. No matter

how long I had been a lady of the night, I had always had to be

high on something. No matter what. Some things you just didn't

get used to. Especially, being forced into that life. Ten minutes

had passed by, and a loud bang interrupted the scenery in the

dining room. Four masked guys, with guns, were busting into

the large mansion. My glass fell out of my hand, breaking into

millions of pieces across the living room floor, as I started

screaming. I hurried and hid behind the huge white leather

sofa, as I covered my head, just in case, they started shooting.

"Everybody get down!" One of the guys yelled, as the

other three gathered things from around the house. I,

immediately, looked over at Janice, and I noticed that she was

sitting there too composed. She had a smirk of amusement on

her face, as she glared across the room at the gunmen. That's

when it all came rushing to me that she was in on it all along! I

guess her homeboy, John, wanted to distract the two rich

Italian men so that he could rob them, but little did they know

that there were three other guys waiting for them on the other

side of the house, killing all four of them, instantly. As soon as

we heard shooting, we dashed out of the house to the car, never

stopping until we reached our destination. Carrie ended up

kicking Janice out of the house for her dishonesty, but

eventually she forgave her, and she was back living with us in

no time. We were grateful to never encounter those guys again.

****

"Shut up, Shut up. If you draw attention over here, I

will start killing everyone in this joint. And, that's a promise,"

Loco whispered in my ear.

I could feel his sweat on the side of my face, so I shut

my mouth, because that didn't have anything to do with anyone else in there. It didn't even have anything to do with me, and

especially, poor Mel. He didn't deserve any of that. I guess, it's

true what people say, "You are the company you keep."

The petite waitress was making her way back to our

table, but I quickly waved her off to give us some more time.

She rolled her eyes in annoyance and walked back towards the

front of the restaurant.

"Okay, everybody calm down. How much does she owe

you?" Melvin asked Loco.

"One-hundred," Loco replied.

"Okay, well I can pay you that," Melvin said, while

reaching for his wallet.

Before he could finish, Loco yelled, "GRAND!" Loco

gave out a loud laugh, giving "Chubby" a high-five. "You have

to be crazy if you think I'm making all of this noise for a

measly hundred," he stated, clenching his gold teeth together.

"Where am I supposed to get that type of money? I got out of the game a long time now," I tried explaining. Melvin gave me a confused look.

"Well, sweetie, that's not my problem," Loco said, as he rubbed his hands across my chin, making every part of my body quiver.

"If you don't have my money by the end of this week, I'm coming to get you just like I got your friend," Loco threatened. I jerked my face from Loco's hand. "Remember what I said. I know you, and I know your family, too. Now you folks have a good day. You hear?" He said, before excusing himself from the table.

My heart went directly to my feet, and I couldn't feel any inch of my body. I froze in disbelief. *I know he did not just admit to killing my best friend, my only friend.* As I stared in disbelief, Melvin grabbed me by my waist and walked me out of the restaurant. As we drove away, there was a moment of complete silence. It was very awkward, at that point, because there was a lot of stuff that was said that I did not want Melvin to know, but I guess the cat let the rat out of the bag!

"So, are you going to tell me what that was all about?" Melvin asked, as he tapped, nervously, on the steering wheel.

God! I did not want to have this conversation right now. I had a million things running through my head at that point. "Where should I start?" I asked.

"You can start by telling me what this guy is talking about. Are you selling drugs? What is it that you are into?" Melvin questioned, as he parked his car in a nearby shopping center.

"No! I mean…. I use to. Look! Don't come up in here judging me! I have enough of that already!" I shouted, as I tied my hair back. All of these questions was making me sweat.

"I'm not judging. I just want to know what is going on so that I can help you," Melvin explained. I guess, I had no choice but to confess my demons, because he was not letting up.

After spilling all of the beans from my past, my present, and everything in between, Melvin had this blank look on his face. "Okay, are you going to say something or are you just going to sit there with that stupid look on your face?" I asked, aggravated.

He looked over at me with his mouth wide open, and said, "Wow! I am so sorry that you have been through all of this alone. I wish that you would have come to me sooner, so that I could have helped you." Melvin tried hugging me, but I wasn't looking for any sympathy.

"Yes, but I was raised to take care of myself," I said, while giving him the cold shoulder.

"I wish you would stop trying to be so guarded and let other people that truly love you take care of you," Melvin stated. Never responding, I folded my arms and faced the window, as I began to count the stars. Ever since I was a kid, I

counted the stars to keep my mind off of the horrible things

that were going on in my life. It was the only way that I coped.

Melvin started up his car and drove me home, never saying

another word about it again. I really needed someone in my

corner, because the people that I dealt with in my life only

brought death to my spirit, but I wasn't going to admit it; I was

only 21 years old, and the last few years of my life had brought

me under. I had been living a life that was bringing me straight

to hell, but how do I come back from there? Where do I start?

How could God ever forgive me?

Later on that night, I went to church where Melvin was

speaking. It felt really good to be in the house of the Lord. As

service was going on, all I kept thinking about was Carrie. No

matter what Carrie and Sam had going on, I still loved Carrie,

and I really missed her so much. I wished that she could have

been there with me like we talked about. She died too young, and I didn't want to be like that. I knew that my life had been really bad and jacked up lately. Some things I brought amongst myself; but what I did from that day forward was up to me. There had to be life after death, right? Church was so good, and Melvin really allowed the Lord to use him. My spirit was feeling renewed for the first time in a long time, but as soon as I arrived home, my spirit was broken, once again. I went home to only find my things thrown out of the house and the locks changed.

"What in the world is going on? I know Janice did not throw my things on the porch and change the locks!" I yelled to myself. "Open up Janice!" I screamed, as I banged on the door.

As I was banging, my next door neighbor, Betty, came outside. Betty informed me that there were a "million" cops at my house a few hours ago. "The landlord came by, kicked everyone out, and changed the locks," Betty stated, as she tightened up her house coat.

"What?! What happened?" I asked, confused.

"I really don't know, but they took some guys away in handcuffs."

Oh! Wow! I thought. "Okay, thanks." She waved and went back into her home. I sat on the steps and placed my head in my hands. All I could think about was where I was going to live until I got back on my feet. I gathered all of my things and headed to the nearest hotel. I called Melvin and told him everything that had happened, and he suggested that I look for a legit job; he would loan me some money until I got back on my feet. After checking into the hotel, I took a long shower to ease my mind. Then, I laid across the bed, said a prayer, and went to sleep. I was all burnt out. I lost my friend, my hustle, and my home. What else was I going to lose...? My mind?

The next morning, I did not want to get up, because I did not sleep well. There was a rain storm going on outside, and it did not make it any better, but could anyone sleep at all with the life that I had? I guessed that it could be worse, even though I didn't really care how worse someone else had it than me. All I knew was that I couldn't get any worse, or else, I was going to break, so I pulled myself up and took a shower. I grabbed my black jeans, my Truck Fit shirt, and my baseball hat. I, then, grabbed an unclaimed umbrella from the hotel lobby, and I was out the door at 9:30 sharp. I went to a couple of places to fill out applications, because I still had "Loco" to tend to, but who was I kidding. None of these penny jobs was going to pay me enough to pay off what he was asking. I had to think of something, and I had to think of it quick. Time was running out, and I needed some fast cash.

Maybe I should call some of my old clients and see if they needed any company, or maybe one of my drug connections had something for me to flip. That was the life that I was trying to avoid, but in order for me to keep my life, that was what I would have to do. After roaming the streets for a few hours, I headed back to the hotel. I didn't mind staying there, because it was discreet and safe, for the most part. Besides, it wasn't too shabby. They served breakfast and dinner every day… something that I never had growing up. I laid my applications on the desk and laid down for a few hours before my appointment with one of my old clients, and before I knew it, I was knocked out.

I turned over to shut off the alarm clock. With one eye open, I noticed that it was 830 p.m., so I pulled myself up and started preparing myself for a night of working. As I was applying my make-up, Melvin called and wanted to have dinner. I declined, because I had a client I had to tend to. Melvin did not have that type of money to give me so why waste my time with him. He was leaving in a couple of days. He was going home and was going to be safe, while I was still here in danger. He seemed disappointed and worried when I told him I had plans, but he would get over it.

"Well, just call me when you have some spare time," Melvin said, dragging his words.

"Okay I will. Say a prayer for me, Melvin, because God doesn't hear mines," I requested.

"God hears you. I think you are the one having trouble hearing him," Melvin responded.

"Maybe so," I said cutting it short. I didn't have time to get into that type of conversation that night. "I will call you tomorrow. Goodnight." There was a brief moment of silence before Melvin responded.

"Goodnight Claudia, and God bless you!"

After dealing with clients after clients and drug after drug, I still didn't have enough by the deadline. All I had was an empty soul. *What am I going to do? I will have to hide away for a few days, but where could I go that I wouldn't be found.* Thoughts began to flood my brain. At that point, it was time to suck up my pride, so I called big sis.

"Hey, Sis!" I said, as soon as Melissa picked up.

"Hey, Claudia, how are you?" Melissa asked.

"I'm doing okay. Look, I wanted to ask you for a
favor.... before I could finish Melissa interrupts me.

"A favor? Look Claudia, I don't have any money to
loan to you right now. I have so many bills, and Gary got a
demotion on his job. I'm sorry," she stated with stress in her
voice.

"Well, maybe I should call you back another time," I
insisted.

"No, no that's okay, I'm listening," she responded. The
stress in her voice made that a lot harder, but I was pretty
desperate.

"First and foremost, I don't need your money." All
though I did, but I wasn't crazy enough to ask for it. I wanted
to know if I could stay with you for a couple of days or just

until I could find me somewhere to live," I asked, nervously,

hoping that she agrees.

"What happened to your place? Did you take my advice

and move out?" Melissa asked, prideful.

"Umm, yes, I sure did," I lied.

"Hold on a minute," Melissa said, placing me on hold. I

guess she put me on hold to consult with her hubby.

Gary is so uptight. I thought to myself, as I rolled my

eyes.

Melissa finally came back on the line after two minutes.

"Okay you can stay, but you will have to stay in the pool

house, because Gary isn't too fond of the idea of someone

living with us," she added.

"Okay, I understand. I'm just happy I will have

somewhere to stay," I said relieved. Besides, who wanted to

stay in the house with her stuck-up husband, Gary? He had

his kid just like him. Gary had custody of his son from a

previous marriage. His ex-wife died in a car accident five

years ago, leaving him to take care of his only son.

CHAPTER 5

For the past few days, I had been laying low and filling out applications online. Even though it seemed like there weren't any jobs in that small town, I had really just been thinking about packing my things and moving far away from there. Just when I decided to take a break from all of the drama in my life and jump into the shower, I got a knock at the door. It was my mother.

"What do you want? You have your nerves showing up here!" I yelled, as I opened the door.

"Well, Claudia, this is Melissa's house, and she invited ME over!" Mother snapped. She held her hand against the door, so I wouldn't close it.

"Well, I don't want to hear anything you have to say, so please step away from the door." Mother stood there for a moment before she decided to cooperate. I slammed the door in her face and continued into the bathroom.

"Claudia, please hear me out!" She banged and yelled from the other side of the door.

Not today devil; I was not going to be provoked into saying things that I should swallow. I blasted my music on high and turned on the shower, but low and behold, when I got out of the shower, Mother was in my bedroom!

"Ma!" I yelled. How did you get in here?" I hurried and covered my body.

"Your sister let me in. She thought that it would be a good idea if we talked, and so do I," she responded.

I give up. Maybe, if I just sit there and allow her to talk, she will leave. "Go ahead, and say what you have to say." I said, as I sat far away from her as possible.

"Where should I start?" She said, as she kicked off her flip-flops and sipped on her coffee. One thing about Mother, after all of the years of drug abuse, she was still a very

beautiful woman. She had the most beautiful hazel eyes that

turned gray in direct sun light. Her skin was the shade of cocoa,

and her hips stuck out just enough to let you know that she was

all woman. "I just want to let you know how sorry I am for all

of the pain that I have caused you. I never meant to hurt you

like I did. I was very mentally sick, and still is."

Before she could continue, I interrupted her. "First of

all!" I said, waving my hand in the air. "I don't know if sick is

the word that I would use." She stood up and came to sit closer

by me.

"Okay Claudia, tell me the word that you would use?"

She asked, as she patted me on my thigh.

"EVIL!" I screamed, as I pushed her hand away from

me.

"Okay, you're right. You have the right to call it

whatever you like. I know that I was not thinking straight. I had a sickness, disease, demon, or whatever you want to call it. All

I know is that I'm paying for it all now."

She went on and on about how she would like for me to

forgive her, but that was very hard to do, when I had so much

resentment in my heart. Strangely, I thought that I would be

able to forgive her more if she would have made my sisters

stand on the street corners and sell themselves, too. Or, if they

would have been molested by one of her men at a very young

age while she was in the next room. It made me feel unloved

and alone. I was really messed up in the head from that, and I

did not know how to escape it all. I closed my eyes and took a

deep breath to calm myself down.

"Well, Mother, that is something that I will have to

bring to the Lord, because he is the only one that can heal the

hurt and the hate that I have deep down inside for you. But, I

do want to ask you something before you go. Something that

has been bothering me for all these years," I said, as I paced my

bedroom floor, with the towel still wrapped around me.

Mother looked up at me with her beautiful, hazel eyes.

"What is it?" She asked, with her hands folded in her lap.

"Why me? I always helped out around the house, and I

never gave any trouble. Why me?" I cried. I tried holding back

my tears, but they continued to fall down my face. Mother

lifted her hand to wipe my tears, but I resisted.

"It wasn't nothing you did wrong, nor right. You was

just there all the time, while your sisters were off at their dads;

you was always home, so I took it out on you," she cried.

"You could have went yourself. You don't know the

pain that I feel constantly. I never really knew how to respect

myself as a woman because of you. Just get out!" I screamed at

the top of my lungs, no longer holding back my composer.

"Wait a minute! I am your mother, and you will listen

to what have to say. I know that you are mad at me for what I put you through, but I'm the one that can't stand to look at

myself in the mirror. I get up in the morning, and I'm

depressed to see sunlight. I believe that God really hates me,

because he keep allowing me to see another day. I can't erase

the past, but I can try and bring about a better future. Many of

times, I wanted to tell Fred to let me go instead of you. I did

say it a time or two, but he would refuse and slap me silly. He

would say how I was washed up, and how you were young and

fresh. He said that I had slept with every pope, preacher, and

priest in town.

There was no one left that wanted me. I went so many

times until I was ruined. No one wanted to deal with me

anymore. I know that that's not an excuse, and God is healing

my brokenness. I just pray that you can forgive me so that you

can be free and move on for yourself. You might think that I

don't love you, but I do, and I'm so sorry." She quickly slipped on her gold flip-flops on and began to walk towards the door. Before closing the door, she sobs, "I am sorry."

As I watched her walk out the door, I wanted to run behind her and hug her, because I knew she was mentally sick, but my pride and resentment didn't let me. Later that day, I called up Melvin to come over and have some lunch with me.

"I'll be there by noon." He agreed to my proposal and arrived shortly afterwards. I was already outside sitting by the pool with my feet in the water. The skies were blue, and there were no clouds in sight. "So what's been going on with you, Miss Lady?" He said, as he reached over to hug me.

"Too much!" I responded.

Melvin chuckled and said, "You, missy, always have something going on." I nodded my head in agreement.

"Yep, never a dull moment with me. I said, winking my eye. Melvin turned his head to hide the fact that he was blushing. "Melvin Joseph Woodman, are you blushing?" I asked, grabbing at his shoulders. Do you still have a crush on

Ms. Claudia?"

Melvin gazed into my eyes. "How couldn't I? You're

smart, beautiful, and most importantly, a God-fearing woman.

Any man would be lucky to have you, and don't you ever think

anything else." I couldn't help but to blush. He was telling me

things that no other man had ever told me before.

"Aww... thanks, Mel. You're so sweet." I leaned in and

gave Melvin a kiss on his cheek. Even though he was saying all

the right things, he was more like a brother to me. Nothing

more and nothing less. It was nice to just sit back and hang out

without any drama for a change.

"So, tell me. What are you going to do about Loco?"

Melvin asked, as he took a bite of the homemade burgers I

whipped up for us.

"I'm going to pay Sam another visit and see if he can

help me," I responded, as I stared into space, while thoughts fluttered through my mind. Melvin stopped eating and directed his attention towards me.

"I don't know, Claudia. Do you think that will work, because he wasn't so happy to see you last time?"

I humped my shoulders. "I don't know, but it can't hurt to try."

Melvin turned to me and grabbed my hands. "How about we pray together about this situation. Let's hear what God is saying." I had never really had anyone sit and pray with me before, but it was different, and it was nice. I began to reminisce back on that day when I had finally decided to go to church instead of the street corner, and I was denied prayer because of the way I was dressed.

****

"When I tell you God is good, God is good. There is no good thing that he will withhold from his faithful servant." The light-skinned pastor preached, as I was walking into the church. The church began to worship and praise from the power in his words, but that was short-lived when they all looked back and noticed me. I was supposed to be working, but instead, I went to church in my street attire. My dress was so short that it almost reached my crouch, and my cleavage was bulging out for every man to see. By the time I would have went home and changed, church would have been over. The Lord said to come as you are, so that's exactly what I did. I sat in the far back so that I wouldn't cause anymore distractions. After service was over, I went up to the pastor for prayer just like the rest of the church.

"Excuse me. Hmm mm. Excuse me?" The old lady behind me said while clearing her throat.

"Yes?" I said, as I turned around to face her.

"Are you okay? Are you lost? The pastor is not interested in "women" like you. Besides, he has a wife and four beautiful children. I don't know who sent you, but Satan get behind thee," she openly rebuked me in front of the church. My face turned red with confusion and embarrassment.

"Ma'am, I don't know what you're implying, but I'm just here like the rest. Jesus is for everybody," I said, with my hands on my hips.

"Young lady!" The pastor called, signaling me with his finger to come see. I walked up to the stage where he preached.

"Yes sir?" I said, as tears fell from my eyes, hoping and praying that God was finally going to set me free.

"I'm sorry, but the way you are dressed, I will not be able to pray for you. The demon that is attached to you is very strong and is not allowed in my church. You must leave immediately, thus says the Lord," he stated, as he pointed towards the doors.

The Lord told him to tell me that? I thought to myself. I

ran out of the church crying. My mother didn't love me, and

now God doesn't either? The way I was denied God's grace

and mercy was the final straw. I stopped believing for a long

time.

****

Tears fell from my eyes, as I reminisced back to that

awful day. After praying with Melvin, he gave me a few bible

verses to read. It felt good… it was like I felt hope again.

Melvin and I sat outside for another hour by the pool laughing

and joking about the good 'ole days.

"Thank you for praying with me, Melvin," I said, as I

kissed him on his cheek.

"Anytime. I want you to be happy. That's all." Melvin hugged me goodnight and let himself out. My day started off rough, but my night ended pretty good. I felt like my spirit was finally healing.

The next morning, I jumped in my car and hit the highway. I needed to solve this little issue with Loco and start living my life. I was faithful to Sam; he owed me. As I was driving up to the prison, I saw the same Monte Carlo that Loco was driving that night when him and "chubby" attacked me.

What is going on? I thought. *Looks like someone snitched on Sam and let Loco know where he was, but why would Loco come to visit Sam? Did he decide to leave me alone and just deal with Sam himself? Is he even here for Sam?* My brain was on overload. I decided to sit in my car and wait to see if Loco would come out before I decided to go in. I didn't want to risk being seen.

A few minutes passed and a voluptuous woman was approaching Loco's car. I rubbed my eyes to make sure that I was seeing what was right in front of me. It was Janice! *What?! Janice knows Loco?* I was really confused and in shock now. I needed some answers, and I needed them quick, so I waited until she left and went in to see Sam. After ten minutes of convincing the security guard to let me in, and promising him a "favor", he finally let me through. When Sam saw me walk through the door, he dropped his head in disappointment.

"Look, Sam, I know you're not happy to see me, but I need your help. I am really in a mess, and it's because of you," I stated, as I held my composer. I was trying not to relive the scenery from the last time that I was there. The awkward feeling, of the fat security guard that was watching me, didn't make it any better.

"What do you mean?" Sam asked, giving me that look that he always gave me when he knew exactly what I was talking about.

"The money you owe Loco. The money that he wants me to pay since you're in jail," I replied.

"I don't know what you are talking about." Sam continued to lie. "Are you done, because I don't have time for questions 101," Sam said, as he stood up to leave.

"What was Janice doing here, Sam?" I asked. His eyes widened, and the look on his face was priceless. He couldn't believe what I had just said. "Yes, that's right! I saw her, so you might as well tell me what's going on, because I am sick of all this drama that I've been going through!" I ranted.

Sam sat back down with his back turned towards me. "I don't know what you are talking about. Besides, you got yourself into this mess. You can't go your whole entire life blaming everyone else," he said.

I swear I wanted to grab him by those dreads and drag

him unto the floor. He never admitted when he was wrong.

"Come on, Sammie. Stop playing these games with me! My

life is on the line here. I thought you really loved me," I begged,

hoping Sam would feel some type of guilt.

"Look, Loco is a dangerous dude, and he don't stop

until he gets what he wants. As far as Janice... Sam finally

turns to face me. She is involved with Loco."

That's why she didn't care what had happened to me

that night. She set me up! I thought to myself. My mind started

racing a mile minute. "So, tell me what did she want?" I asked,

impatiently.

"She came by looking for answers of your

whereabouts." I told her that I didn't know and that she should

never come to visit me again," Sam responded.

"And, the money? Why do you owe Loco that much

money?" I asked, irritated.

He took a moment before he decided to answer. Sam whispered, "About two years ago, we had a drug deal that was supposed to break an even one-hundred thousand. The deal went bad, and since it was my idea, he blamed me. He found the guys that didn't come through with the deal and killed them both. And, now it's like he's trying to kill everyone that's close to me. Thank God my mom and pops are already gone." Sam makes a sign of a cross across his chest. *But, if that's the case, why am I still living?* I thought to myself.

"Well, this doesn't have anything to do with me!" I barked. The fat security guard looked towards me and signaled for me to be quiet. I rolled my eyes and redirected my attention back to Sam.

"What you don't understand? As long as you are involved with me or was involved, you are just as dead as me," Sam specified. It was like someone had hit me in the stomach with a ton of bricks and knocked the wind out of me.

What am I going to do? What did I get myself into? Sam was useless. I did not have anyone that could help me. I sure didn't want to involve Melvin and take him to hell with me. I am at my wits end. My mind began to battle. I got up and left from the table without saying another word. I left the jail feeling as though my days were numbered.

CHAPTER 6

My visit with Sam had only made me feel worse. I was
more mixed up on what I needed to do in order to save my life.
Sam's words replayed in my head over and over again. I
couldn't eat or think. As I was lying across my bed, thoughts of
Melvin flashed before me. I remembered the bible verses that
he had given me to read on the other night. I reached into the
nightstand to grab my bible. As I began to read the bible verses
and worship God, I felt a sense of peace rush over me. I could
hear the words in my spirit "I AM with you." All I could do
was cry, because I knew, at that very moment, that God was
with me.

I hadn't felt his presence like that in a long time. All I
had to do was push away my pride and tear down some walls,
and I was able to hear him. I was the one hindering my ears all
this time. Many times in life, we feel as though God is not

there, but all the while, he has been speaking to us. In that very

moment, I knew that my life was changed. I knew that I could

finally see. All the madness that had been going on, I decided

to give to Jesus. I couldn't handle it on my own. I submitted.

After waking up the next morning from a good night's

sleep. Melissa was knocking at my door.

"Hey sissy, are you up? I would like to speak to you

about a few things." I opened the door to let her in.

"Yes, come on in. I'm just waking up. Did you have any

coffee this morning? I can fix us some," I asked, as I walked

past her to the kitchen.

"That would be nice!" Melissa said, with a smile.

"So, what is it that you want to talk about?" I asked, as I

poured her a cup of Starbucks brand coffee.

"Is everything okay?" She asked, worried. I couldn't

hide it anymore. I just had to let her know.

"No," I said, as I handed her a cup of coffee.

"Go on," Melissa said, readily.

"I got myself caught up with the wrong people, and now, they want me to pay them 100 thousand dollars, or I am dead!" I sobbed. Tears began to flow.

"Oh no, Claudia! I'm so sorry that you are going through this alone. We have our differences and all, but you are my sister, and I love you dearly. Melissa reached over to give me a hug. I suppressed my face into her chest and released all of the stress that I had been carrying.

"I just don't know what to do! I tried everything," I said, as I pulled myself together.

"What are the people's names that are threatening your life?" She asked, as she sipped on her hot coffee.

"Well, there is this guy that goes by the name of Loco, and then, there is this other chubby looking guy, but I don't know his name. Then, there is Janice.... Melissa interrupts me.

"Wait! Janice who? The one you was living with?"

Melissa's face turned beet red.

"Yes, the one I was living with," I replied.

"I can't believe this!" Melissa yelled and hit her fist

against the table. "Darn snake in the grass! I will get to the

bottom of this, trust me. I will look through a few databases to

see if I can get this Loco guy's real name and see what he is all

about. I will see if he has any warrants for his arrest, and I will

take him in. Meanwhile, you just lay low and try to avoid going

places that they may be," Melissa instructed.

"Okay. I will," I agreed.

"Oh! Look at the time! I will be late for work if I don't

get out of here. Will you be okay by yourself?" Melissa

questioned, as she scrambled around looking for her keys.

"Yes, I will be fine," I reassured her.

"Okay. See you later, and remember what I said," Melissa stated. I nodded my head and waved her off. Melissa winked and walked out.

I took my sister's advice and stayed in. Besides, it gave me some time to catch up on my bible studies. I felt really peaceful when I read my bible, and that was how I wanted to stay, but the Devil wasn't too far behind to mess that up. Later on that day, I received a text message from Janice stating for me to call her. Her text read,

Janice: I been really down about Carrie lately, and I need someone to talk to. Please call me.

Wow! I thought. She had her nerves! What was her motive? What tricks did she have up her sleeves? But, then again, maybe I should give her a call. I decided to give Janice a call and pretend that I didn't know anything.

"Hello, Janice," I stated, as she answered.

She was really trying to make herself seem so sad about Carrie. I had to wonder if she even cared about her death after all.

"Hey, Claudia, thanks for calling me back. I know we haven't been the best of friends." I interjected.

"Or friends at all," I stated.

"No don't say that! We were friends at one point, and with Carrie being gone, I would like for us to get that back. Maybe we could get together and talk about a fundraiser to help pay for her funeral expenses," Janice proposed.

She really was a snake in the grass just like Melissa said. She could have been an actress the way she was performing, but I would let her think that she was smart and that I was imprudent to what her and Loco was up to.

"Well, I have been busy lately. I flew out of town for a couple of days after the funeral to clear my head. I'm in Detroit, visiting some family that I've recently discovered on my dad's

side of the family," I lied.

There was a brief moment of silence before Janice

decided to respond. "Oh, really? When did you find this out?"

Janice asked, shocked.

"A couple of days ago as a matter of fact. I never met

up with my dad, but I did meet up with some of my aunts and

uncles," I continued to lie. "But, I will be back down by the

weekend. I shall call you, and we can meet up for some lunch,"

I suggested.

"Sounds good!" Talk to you soon!" Janice said, as she

hung up the phone. I just fed Janice some good 'ole steak and

potatoes. I bet she thought that she was so full that she was

about to burst. In reality, though, she was still starving. I

needed to let my sister know what was going on, right away!

Before I could make it to the back door of Melissa's

house, she was walking towards the pool house.

"Hey, Melissa, were you able to find out anything?" I asked, as I met her outside by the pool.

"Yes, I was just about to come by the pool house and let you know what I've found out. First off, this "Loco" guy is a twenty-seven-year-old, named Terrence Bird. He has been to jail multiple times for drug possession. He served five years in prison. He has been out for a few months now." Melissa took a deep breath. "Listen, Claudia, Loco is known to murder; he just hasn't been caught yet. In the past, he was known to run with a guy they called "Brick". He is described exactly the way you described his friend that he has been rolling with. His real name is Roy James. He is twenty-five-years-old. He has also been to jail for drug possession. I looked into Janice, too, but her record is clean." Melissa carried on, as she looked through her paperwork.

"So is Loco wanted for arrest?" I asked, as I paced the patio floor.

"Yes he is. He was spotted at a recent home invasion two weeks ago, so I'm pretty certain that that is why he is after that money so much," Melissa responded.

"What do you mean?" I questioned.

"I don't think this has anything to do with Sam like he thinks it does," Melissa said, as she looked up for a second from her paperwork.

"Loco is trying to flee far away from here as soon as possible, because he knows that, if he goes back to jail, that will be the end for him." The thought of Loco in jail made me smile.

"So what's next? How do we stop him in his tracks?" I asked.

"I don't know just yet, but I'm working on it, Sis," Melissa said, as she flipped through her paperwork some more. I reached over to grab my phone.

"There is probably something that we can do. I received a text message from Janice the other day. She was saying how she was so "sad" about Carrie and how she needed someone to talk to. Maybe you can set me up with your friends at the FBI, and I can meet up with her and bust her and Loco," I proposed.

"Oh! I don't know if that's a good idea, Claudia. That would be too dangerous, and I can't afford to lose you." Melissa stood up and closed her briefcase.

"I know that you are worried, but I have to end this once and for all. I am tired of running away. I've been running away my whole life, and I haven't gotten anywhere. Please let me do this. This way, the streets can be a little safer, and Carrie and her family can have some type of justice," I pleaded, as I followed Melissa towards the main house.

Melissa stopped walking, stared at me, and said, "You were always so independent and strong."

I grabbed Melissa's hand. "That's because I've been through so much, Sis, and I had no choice but to be. Even though mommy wasn't there for me, nor my dad, God has always kept me. He was always a friend to me when I wasn't a friend to myself. He allowed me to go through so that I would be able to do what I'm doing today. Now, I'm starting to understand my journey and my destiny. Melissa smiled and hugged me.

"Well, Sissy, let's bring justice to the table! Oh, and Sis, I know we lost a lot of time when my daddy took me away, but we have now," Melissa stated, as she walked into the house.

****

"You're not taking my child nowhere! Take your hands off of me!" My mother shouted, as child custody was escorting

Melissa out of the house. I stared from the doorway, with tears in my eyes, as I watched Melissa being pulled into freedom. My heart beat with jealousy. The way my mother yelled and screamed made my stomach turn, even though I knew it was only because she was losing her money instead of her daughter.

"I'm sorry," Melissa whispered, as the tall, white lady escorted her out the front door.

Iyanna ran towards the door, and cried. "Please don't take my sister."

My mother grabbed Iyanna by her arm and swung her into the kitchen. "Shhh, baby don't cry. If you cry they will take you away, too. You don't want that, right?"

Mother bent down to Iyanna's size, giving her complete eye contact and manipulation.

"No, mommy," Iyanna said, as she wiped her eyes.

"Come on, I will fix you a big pan of Lasagna. Iyanna,

only being nine at the time, didn't know any better. On the

other hand, I was reaching thirteen, and I knew what kind of

mother she was.

"Come here, Yanna. Let's get you cleaned up for

dinner," I said, giving my mother an evil gaze.

Mother folded her arms and gave a slight grin... Just

enough to let me know that she was the devil. It was a hard

knock life for us. The night they took Melissa was the night my

soul died.

CHAPTER 7

Friday came, and I was pretty much getting nervous at
that point. It was time to put an end to it all. I was just hoping
for the best.

"Hey, Claudia, did you call Janice yet? Melissa asked,
as she walked into my room.

"Not yet. Oh, God! Melissa, I am so nervous, and I did
not sleep much at all last night. I hope I'm making the right
decision," I said, while biting my nails.

Delight filled Melissa's face. "You can always back out,
you know."

She's probably right. Maybe, this isn't such a good idea.
I thought to myself. I, immediately, shook my thoughts away.
"No! I will do it. No more backing out," I shouted, as I paced
the floor.

Melissa grabbed my arm. "Could you stop? You

making me nervous." We looked at each other and laughed.

"Did you talk to Iyanna and let her know what's going

on?" I asked.

"I did, and she was asking to be there, but I told her that

it would be too dangerous," Melissa replied, as she plopped

down on the bed.

"Yes, that's for the best. So, are you ready to do this?"

Melissa nodded her head.

"And, put it on speaker phone," Melissa demanded,

pointing her finger towards my phone. I reached over to grab

my phone to call Janice. After the second ring, Janice answered

the phone.

"Hey girl, I didn't think you was going to call." Janice

said, with relief in her voice.

"Hey! Yeah, I just got back into town," I pretended. "So

are we still meeting up?" In my heart, I was somewhat hoping that she would decline, because my nerves were getting the best of me.

"Yes, I was thinking we could have lunch at my apartment." Melissa rolled her eyes at Janice's comment. I shook my head in amusement.

This heifer is trying to set me up! But she about to have a rude awakening.

"Umm, I was thinking that, since we are getting together to discuss Carrie, we could meet up at her favorite spot. You know, that nice little Mexican restaurant across town," I recommended. I turned towards Melissa and winked my eye. Melissa smiled and gave me the thumbs up. There was a brief moment of silence. For a second, I thought that she had hung up. "Hello?" I said.

"I'm here. I guess, guess that would be okay," she stuttered. "I really don't like Mexican food, but since it's about her, it will be fine," she agreed.

"Great! I will see you at 5-ish?" She agreed before hanging up.

"I can't believe she think I'm that stupid to go to her house!" I said. Melissa and I laughed.

"Well, it seems as though everything is going as planned," Melissa stated.

"Yes, we will see how it goes," I said, as I stretched across my bed. "I think I will close my eyes until later." I was mentally exhausted.

A little later that morning, Melvin came by to let me know that he was leaving town. "I can't believe you are leaving so soon!" I said, as I gave him a huge hug.

"I know. Neither can I, but I will be back next month to check on my aunt. She hasn't been feeling too well lately, and I'm concerned about her. Will you be alright?" Melvin asked with concern. I didn't bother mentioning the meeting that I'd scheduled with Janice, because if I did, he would have stayed.

He shouldn't put his life on hold, because of me.

"Don't worry about me. I will be just fine. You have

been such a blessing to me. You have opened my eyes to things

that I was blind to for many years. It was no mistake that you

came back into my life when I was at my lowest. You are truly

a friend," I said, patting him on his back.

Melvin leaned in to kiss me on my forehead, and said,

"Too bad I'm just a friend, because I really do care about you."

Really and truly, I was afraid of love, because almost everyone

in my life that I did love or claimed to have loved me, managed

to hurt me. My heart could not take that type of friction

anymore. I had to heal.

"Only God knows Mel, only God knows!" Melvin gave

a slight grin and left. I was really going to miss him, but I had

bigger things to think about. It was time to get down to

business. Next stop, Janice and Loco!

Five o'clock came around, and my heart was pounding. I was all set up with the equipment that Melissa got from one of her FBI friends. I had a hidden wire so that Melissa could hear everything that was going on. Melissa and I decided that my code word would be "Loyal", just in case, I needed her to call the cops. Melissa decided to lay low at the burger joint right across the way from the restaurant.

When I arrived at the restaurant, Janice hadn't yet arrived. I was pretty sure that her and Loco were outside making sure that the coast was clear. That gave me the advantage of where I wanted to be seated. I made sure I sat in the far back by the open window, so that I would be in clear view for Melissa. The restaurant was nice and quiet, and there were barely anyone there. That was perfect just in case something had to pop off. About fifteen minutes later, Janice finally arrived. She strolled in wearing all white. She had on a fake mink collar around her neck and a large white hat. I guess

she thought she was the first lady of the mafia or something.

"Hey, girl. How have you been? It's good to see you,"

Janice said, while wiggling her hips, with the fakest smile

placed on her lips. Janice had to be on some sort of drugs,

because her eyes were blood shot red.

"Hey hunni. I am good. Is everything okay? Your eyes

are red?" I asked, pointing at her eyes.

"No, girl, that's just my allergies," she indicated.

Yeah right! I know the difference between being stoned

and having itchy eyes. I thought to myself while rolling my

eyes.

Janice reached into her fake matching mink purse and

grabbed her eye drops. Dropping two drops in each eye.

"Let's sit," I said, as I pulled out my chair. Janice

looked around the room to scope out the scenery before sitting

down. The tall, handsome waiter was coming our way, but I

signaled for him to give us a minute. I did not need any
distractions.

"So, tell me what it is that you want to discuss
concerning Carrie?" I asked, as I studied her body language.

"Well, I was thinking that we could do a fundraiser to
help her family pay for the funeral. I heard from one of
Carrie's cousin's that they had to take out a loan to pay for it,"
Janice said, while looking at the menu.

All I could do was laugh to myself, because that was a
lie. Carrie's family was not suffering in that area at all. Carrie
just got with the wrong crowd.

"Okay, so what were you thinking?" Maybe a dinner or
a garage sale?" I played along.

She looked up at me with a devilish grin on her face, as
she placed the menu on the table. "I, myself, was thinking
about a ransom…. for your life in exchange for 100 thousand
dollars!" Janice said, as her devilish grin turned into a frown. I

adjusted my button on my shirt, because the heat was definitely

rising.

"I beg your pardon?"

"You heard me! If you make one move, Loco will blow

your head clean off your shoulders," Janice said, as she

gnashed her teeth.

"Loco?!" I said, acting flabbergasted.

"What do you and Loco have to do with each other?" I

said, as I waved the waiter away one last time, but he continued

to walk in our direction anyway.

"Ma'am, will you be ordering soon? There are other

people that are waiting for a seat," the handsome waiter, asked

irritated.

"Yes, I am sorry. We cannot make up our minds." I

pointed back and front between Janice and I. "Just bring us a

couple of waters please," I responded.

The tall waiter rolled his eyes in frustration and walked away. Ignoring his attitude, I directed my attention back towards Janice.

"So, do you know Loco?" I questioned, as if I didn't know.

"Oh that's right, you don't know." Janice said, slightly placing her hand on my shoulder. Loco is my lover, my main thing, my man, or whatever you want to call it. We've been planning this for some months now. I am the one that set Sam up. We had to get him out of the way so that we wouldn't have any distractions."

At that point, I wanted to jump over the table and claw her eyes out, but I had to stay in character, so I continued to play victim. Removing her hand from my shoulder, I said, "And...Carrie? Did you have anything to do with her death?"

Afraid of the answer that I might receive, my heart
began to race, as the question rolled from my tongue. Janice
took a while before she answered me.

"Of course not. She was just in the wrong place at the
wrong time," Janice said, as she stared down at the table. I
guess that's what Loco told her, but he did exactly what he
wanted to do, and that was kill her.

"I can't believe you! You was supposed to be my friend.
I was there for you through a lot of your struggles. Where am I
supposed to get that type of money?!" I yelled, leaning in
towards her.

"First of all, lower your tone before things get really
messy in here," Janice said, in a demanding tone, as she studied
the room.

"Well, I don't have that type of money," I stated.

"But your perfect, beloved sister, Melissa, does," Janice
implied.

"Oh, you are way over your head! Melissa does not have that type of money," I reassured.

My legs began to shake, and my body tensed up. I didn't know how much longer I would be able to hold it together. Janice had my blood boiling, and I was only seconds away from pulling her throat out. Janice laughed and shook her head.

"You don't think I know about the baby that she loss, and how she sued the hospital for malpractice?"

I couldn't believe what I was hearing from this no good snake. This had to be their plan all along. What other reason would they come after me for that type of money?

"How do you even know about that?" I asked in frustration. Janice, seductively, licked her lips, and said, "Gary!" She gave out a loud laugh that made me nauseous. I was so disgusted with it all.

"Just stop it! Just stop it! This is between us and no one else," I demanded. It felt as though smoke was coming from my nostrils, as I stared at Janice with detestation. There were rumors of Janice and Gary fooling around, but I never really fed into it, because the streets were always talking, and some things, you just couldn't trust.

"You leave my family out of this, Jezebel!" I said, as I stood up to walk away, because things were going completely left field.

Janice quickly stood up and said, "I suggest that you sit down, or you will get shot down," she mumbled.

"No, I'm out of here! You have wasted enough of my time. You and your so-called man can go straight to hell with the rest of the devils!"

As I was grabbing my purse to leave, Janice grabbed my arm. "Lil Mama, I suggest that you sit down or that laser that's directed right in-between your chest will blow your insides completely out," she said, tapping her finger into my chest.

I looked down at my shirt, and there it was… a laser light right in the middle of my chest.

"What is that?!" I panicked.

"That's what's going to hit you if you don't shut your mouth and do exactly what I tell you to do." Janice pushed me back down in my seat.

"Listen up! You are going to go to your sister, and you are going to get her checkbook. You are going to write out a check for 100 thousand dollars. When you write the check, you will write it out for Cash," she demanded, as she was becoming irritated.

"You will never get away with this!" I said, uncertainly.

Janice chuckled, "For the sake of your life, and the people that you love, we better!"

As my mind began to race, I wasn't sure if I should say the code name or not. Loco was out there somewhere watching everything. I was too afraid to put my life in jeopardy and everyone else's. I would just have to settle this at another time and location. All I knew was that time was running out. Janice pulled her chair from the table and stood up.

"Oh, before you think about leaving town, again. Just know that we are watching." She grabbed her purse and walked out.

I, immediately, looked down at my chest when she walked away hoping that the red light was gone, but it stayed there for another five minutes. I sat there with sweat dripping from my pores. My body became plagued with fear, as I said a silent prayer, asking God to forgive me for all of the wrong that I had done. I had all types of emotions raging through my body. The things that Janice just revealed tonight just took the game to a whole other level. Time was running out. I sat at the table for a few more minutes before the handsome waiter was

walking in my direction.

"Is everything okay?" He asked worried. Before

answering, I looked down at my chest, and the light was gone.

I sighed in relief.

"Yes, I'm just fine," I replied, without looking in his

direction, and got up from the table. I guess he was pretty

concerned, because he followed me to the door.

"Thank you, Ma'am. Have a good night…be careful out

there," He added. I nodded my head, gave a slight smile, and

walked out.

CHAPTER 8

After leaving the restaurant, my thoughts were racing a mile a minute.

"Claudia!" My sister came running towards me.

"Are you okay?!"

All I could do was collapse in her arms. I had never had this overwhelming feeling before in my life. It felt as though I was about to lose my mind. All of this felt so surreal.

"Did you hear everything?" I asked between sobs. She looked at me with tears in her eyes.

"I heard it all." I reached over and grabbed her hand. The look on Melissa's face was so indescribable. She grabbed my hand and held on real tight, but it wasn't just sadness that I saw in her eyes. There was rage, as well.

"I'm so sorry, Melissa." Melissa resisted the pity.

"No, I will be okay. It will all be okay. Gary hasn't seen nothing yet. He will be sorry his behind ever existed. Let's focus on what's really important and that's putting an end to all of this madness," she said, as we walked towards her car. Melissa nervously searched for her keys in her purse before she was able to find them.

"Hey, sissy, I know that Gary is a fool and all, but don't do anything stupid just because he doesn't know how to keep it in his pants," I stated.

Melissa never responded and started up the car. On the ride back to her house, Gary kept blowing up her phone.

"What! If you see I'm not answering, why do you keep trying?" Melissa yelled into her phone. Melissa pressed the end button and tossed it into the back seat. "Stupid men," Melissa mumbled. She was completely silent on the ride back to her place. Every time she was quiet like that, an explosion was about to happen. As soon as we arrived to her house, Gary's no

good behind was waiting for her on the porch.

"What's the matter with you?" Gary asked, worried.

"You know what's wrong. Go reread the text messages

that I sent your black behind earlier." Melissa shoved her

finger into Gary's forehead.

"Baby, I told you that that's not true," Gary swore.

Melissa rushed into the house and grabbed a few of her things.

"I will be sleeping in the pool house, and your trifling

behind better stay away from me, or I promise you that things

will get real ugly," Melissa threatened.

I pulled Melissa by her arm. I was so sick of all of the

drama. Gary continued to yell meaningless words, as we

walked towards the pool house. He paced back and forth all

night between the pool house and their house. Melissa slept on

the couch with her 9 mm underneath her pillow. She said she

was just being cautious. It was the first night that I saw my mother in Melissa. I truly believed that she wanted Gary to come through that door starting his mess. A woman scorned could be a man's nightmare. I couldn't sleep as I thought about her gun underneath her pillow. I stayed up most of the night drinking coffee and energy drinks just to stay up. I was destined not to allow the same thing to happen to Gary that happened to Joe.

****

"The more you make, the less I see," My mother yelled at unlucky number 9. My mother went through men like she went through toilet paper.

"My money is my money. If you want more money, go trick on the corner like you do. I'm not giving my money to no street walker," Joe slurred, as he tripped over one of Iyanna's

baby dolls, which she left from the last time we all stayed at

Joe's.

Joe wasn't a rich man, but he was doing okay for

himself. He owned his own trucking company. He built him a

three bedroom house on a huge lot. When he first met my

mother, he was all together. After a year with her, he started

drinking heavily, and he stayed drunk twenty-four seven. I

guess staying sober around her was like pulling teeth. She

brought every good man down. Before he could stand up, my

mother hurried and grabbed one of the vases from the cabinet

and smashed it across Joe's head. He collapsed onto the floor,

and I thought he was dead, for a second, until he started to

moan while holding his head.

"Yes, that will teach you to mess with me." My mother

grabbed an iron bat that was standing in the corner and

knocked Joe across his back. He gave out a loud groan. I

covered my eyes, as I became terrified. I was, once again,

alone with that unstable creature. Times like that, I really
needed my sisters.

"Where is the money?!" She yelled, as she pounded the
bat across his back. His body jumped with every blow.

"God help me," Joe groaned.

"God, God?" My mother laughed. "God doesn't hear
you. You are nothing. You are the servant of the devil." She
continued to laugh. She threw the bat in the corner and ran
into the kitchen. I hurried and followed behind her to see what
she was up to. She was hunting around his cabinet drawers like
a mad woman with her hair all over her head. By the time she
found what she was looking for, Joe was already behind her in
the kitchen. He swung at her missing her head by an inch. My
mother grabbed the smallest knife off of the cabinet and started
to jab it continuously into Joe's side.

"Stop! Momma! Stop!" I cried and screamed,
hysterically. Joe became faint and fell to the floor. She grabbed

my hand, and we fled away from Joe's apartment. Ten minutes

later, we arrived to a nearby crack house. After entering the

dark and smelly abandoned house, she instructed me to sit and

not to move. She disappeared into one of the rooms in the back

with some strange man. I heard her shouting and making

claims that Joe attacked her and that he needed to go over and

finish him off. A few minutes later, my mother and the strange

man came out of the room. She was fixing her clothes and

wiping her mouth.

"Look, you stay here. I have something that I need to

take care of," she said, grabbing my face.

"I don't want to stay here by myself," I cried. I was

only eleven years old, and she wanted to leave me in a crack

house. I couldn't believe that a mother would do such a thing

to her child.

"I said I will be back," she said, pointing her finger against my nose. *"Look,"* she pointed towards a big hole in the wall. *"Hide in there; I will be back in ten minutes."*

I guess that was her way of showing compassion. I ran and sat in the hole, and I cried, nonstop, until she returned.

Her clothes were filled with blood. "Mommy, what's that?" I asked.

"Come on." She jerked at my arm. "You didn't see nothing, and you bet not say nothing." We walked back to our apartment, and that was when I knew the true definition of a woman's scorned.

****

The next morning, when I woke up, Melissa was already gone. I jumped out of my bed and ran to check if

Melissa's gun was still under her pillow, and it was gone. I

grabbed my slippers and walked towards the main house. My

dreams and my past had me paranoid. I walked around to the

window by their bedroom to see if I could hear anything. I

decided not to go in, because I was afraid of what I might see,

but I overheard Gary and Melissa fussing about the night

before.

"This is all Claudia's fault," Gary made accusations.

Just like a typical man; always blaming someone else

for their mess. I thought to myself while shaking my head.

"Grab your clothes, and get out, before I do something

that I may or may not regret," Melissa threatened.

"Fine. I'm out," Gary said.

I waited five minutes to go inside after Gary left to

make sure that he was really gone. I could see how much that

that was affecting Melissa, but she wasn't going to say. She

had her game face on, and she was ready to end the mess that I was in. Besides, it was her job to track the bad guys and to

bring them in.

"Will you be okay?" I asked, as I poured myself a bowl

of Cinnamon Toast Crunch.

"Yeah I'm okay." Melissa said, as she buttoned her

blouse. My phone vibrated, causing me to look down at my

screen; I had received a text...

Janice: I'm still watching you.

It was from Janice. I turned off my phone and

continued to eat my cereal. I didn't bother telling Melissa,

because she had enough on her plate already.

"Okay, girl, I'm heading to work. Just try to stay here.

Mom is coming by to pick up some things that she left, so if

you run into her, please be nice," Melissa said, grabbing her

keys from the key rack on the wall. I looked at her with a
frown.

"I will try." Melissa shook her head and rolled her eyes.

"Okay, sis," Melissa laughed. "The police are looking
for Loco and Janice right now; we will find them sooner are
later. We have to get those two off the streets and get you safe
again."

I looked at Melissa, and said, "There is no weapon that
is formed against me that shall prosper. My life is in his hands
now." She smiled, as she headed out the door.

The thought of Loco and Janice made me sick to my
stomach. After five minutes of involuntarily vomiting up the
Cinnamon Toast Crunch that I had just consumed, I decided to
call Melvin up to see how he was doing.

"Hello sweetheart," Melvin flirted, as he answered.

"Hey, Mr. Melvin. How are you today?" I responded.

"I'm doing better now since I'm hearing your voice," he continued to flirt.

Melvin was really on ten today. I didn't know if he was struck by cupid, but he needed to come back down off of cloud nine. I brushed off his flirting, because I had things going on, and becoming romantically involved with Melvin, was not on my list. After updating Melvin about the meeting that I had with Janice, there was a brief moment of silence.

"Hello?" I asked. I just knew he was upset.

"Yes?" Melvin responded.

"Well, didn't you hear what I said?" I questioned.

"Yes, I heard you. I just want to know, why didn't you let me know all of this before I left? I could have stayed around to help." Melvin finally answered, a bit irritated.

"There wasn't anything for you to do. Besides, my sister was with me. I was safe. Your prayers are helping tremendously. Don't stop praying for me," I stated.

"I won't ever stop. Just don't stop praying for yourself," Melvin replied.

"So, Melvin, when are you coming back into town?" I asked, quickly changing the subject.

"I will be in town in two weeks," Melvin replied.

I was so excited to hear him say that, because I needed some positive vibes around me with everything that had been going on.

"That's good, because I'm really missing your positive vibe," I said.

"That's nice to hear, Claudia, which means a lot to me. Take care of yourself and stay away from trouble. You hear me?" Melvin instructed, with a firm tone.

"Yes my "Father", I hear you," I said, jokingly.

"Ha! Okay, I will talk to you soon." He hung up.

After hanging up with Melvin, my mom was
approaching the house. I tried to hide, but somehow, she saw
me.

"Claudia! Are you trying to avoid me?" She said, as she
entered the kitchen.

"Duh," I mumbled under my breath. "What's up, Mom?
How is everything? Are you still in treatment?" I asked, but
didn't really want an answer.

"Well..." before she could finish, I knew what she was
going to say.

"Don't tell me you left the program. I just knew it! You
don't care about nobody but yourself." I rolled my eyes and
walked into the living area.

"No, no. I left, because I have been doing really well,
and I wanted to be home. I missed being home," she stated, as
she followed me into the living area.

"I don't even care anymore, Mom. Do what you want.
Anyway, Melissa said you was coming by to pick up some of
your things?" I asked, as I straightened up the throw pillows
that was on the chaise.

Staring at the floor, she looked up at me and said, "I
was thinking about asking her if I could stay here for a little
while, just until my apartment comes through."

Oh, heck no! I thought to myself. *There is no way I am
staying here with her! I left her years ago, and I don't want to
replay that all over again.*

"Wait! What?! You cannot stay here. There is no room
for you. Besides, Gary is not letting you live here," I said, as I
gathered her things.

"Melissa called me this morning and said that Gary will
not be staying here for a while, just until they work some
things out. What is the problem, Claudia? I thought we moved

past things," Mother said, as she grabbed her belongings from me.

"Look, it's not that easy to move on. I'm learning to forgive you and all, but the wounds are still there, and I don't want anything to trigger them again," I replied.

"I understand, but I really need a place to stay. I promise to stay out of your way." She promised, as she grabbed the TV remote and started flipping through the channels. I rolled my eyes in frustration. I couldn't do that. I did not have the energy to fight with her about it. I still had Loco and Janice watching my every move.

"Whatever! That is between you and Melissa. This is not my house. I'm going back to the pool house. See you later." I said, as I walked out of the kitchen door. I did not have time to go back and forth with her over something that I could not control.

Later that evening, I received an anonymous phone call.

"Hello?" I answered.

"Time is ticking, or I will be picking y'all off one-by-one with my silver tone gun." It was Loco! He gave out an evil laugh.

"The police will get you, and you will never get away with this!" I yelled through the phone.

"You better have my money by Thursday or your little sister will be six feet under!" He threatened, as he hung up.

My heart began to race. I had to warn Iyanna! I hurried and grabbed my phone to call her.

"Come on, Iyanna. Pick up!" I said, nervously, shaking my legs. She wasn't answering her phone, so I jumped into my car and sped down the interstate. About thirty minutes later, I arrived at her house. It took me a minute to get there, because Iyanna stayed in the next town over. As I was knocking on the door, I could hear loud wrestling sounds coming from the inside. I tried getting in, but the door was locked.

"Iyanna! Iyanna are you okay?!" I yelled in a panic. I had to get in there some way, somehow. I looked around for anything that I could get my hands on, and I grabbed the biggest rock that I saw and threw it into the window. As I was entering the house, I seen movement coming from the back room. I slowly walked towards the hallway, and I called out for my sister.

"Iyanna? Are you okay?" My heart was racing a mile a minute.

God, please do not let me find her dead. I prayed. There was no answer. I continued to pace myself down the hall. The next thing I knew, I was waking up in my own blood in the hallway. I had a huge gash across my forehead. I tried to get up, but I stumbled back onto the floor. My vision was quite blurry, as I looked around to see if the coast was clear. It was empty, and there was no sign of Iyanna anywhere. She was gone!

Once my vision became clear, I immediately dialed 911! Still shook up, I managed to call Melissa, as well. She was hysterical when I told her what had happened. Twenty minutes later, the ambulance and the cops arrived. All the neighbors were outside watching and whispering amongst themselves. The police questioned them to see if anyone had seen anything, but of course, they denied seeing anything at all. *Where were they when my sister was being kidnapped?* I thought to myself.

The paramedic lifted me into the van and sped off. When I arrived at the local hospital, Melissa was already there waiting for me.

"Melissa!" I cried. I'm so sorry. This is all my fault!" I reached for her, as I laid in the stretcher.

"Hush, now, girl. This is no one's fault but the fools that did this. You have to give yourself a break."

Wiping my tears, I looked up at her, and said, "Is she dead?" If Iyanna was dead, I would never forgive myself.

"No, they wouldn't do that. I mean...not just yet. I know their type. This is all about the money. We will find her, and we will bring her back," Melissa responded, latching onto my hand.

"I just want to die. Maybe I can call a few of my clients and see if there is someone that is willing to pay that much. I will do whatever they want, it does not matter! I just want my sister back!" I cried.

"Claudia, please stop talking like that. No one is going to sell themselves anymore! You hear me? You don't have to go back to that life every time things get rough for you. You will have to learn how to deal with problems like normal people. We pray our way out. Now, I said everything will be okay. I want you to believe in me and have faith," Melissa said, as she wiped my tears.

"I'm just so tired," I said.

There was a price to pay for everything. It seemed good at the moment, but all the bad things you've done comes right back around. A few minutes later, the nurse took me into a private room to do to a CAT scan just to make sure I wasn't bleeding internally. She checked my vitals, supplied me with some meds, and prompted me to rest. After a few hours of being questioned by the police, I was released from the hospital, with a mild concussion and a few stitches. Melissa suggested that the detectives come by the house tomorrow when I would be feeling more up to par.

"You will be staying with me tonight. That way, I can keep an eye on you," Melissa insisted, as she helped me into the car.

"Sounds good," I agreed. I laid my head back onto the seat and closed my eyes the rest of the ride home. Just when we were settling in, the drama started. My mother was approaching the house. By the way she moved when she walked, I could tell that she had it on her mind to start some

drama.

"I can't believe you!" Mother screamed, as she

bombarded her way through the door. "This is all your fault!

You got yourself into some mess, and you brought everyone

along for the ride. She motioned her hand, as if she was driving.

Now, your sister is missing!" She screamed, as she pointing her

finger in my face.

I, quickly, took a step back, because she was a little too

close for comfort. The way my heart was set up for her, I was

liable to slap the mess out of her and think about it later. "You

have your nerves! You have no room to say the things that you

are saying! You had me up and all through the streets so you

could feed your high, and where were you while I was being

molested by your MEN!" I shouted. I shouted so hard that I had

to catch my balance, in which I became dizzy.

Melissa had the oddest look on her face. "Wait!"

Melissa said, while shaking her head in disbelief. "What?" The

look on Mother's face was priceless. She started pacing back

and forth, as though she was about to go into a panic attack.

Melissa knew I gave pleasure to men in return for some cash,

but what she didn't know was that it originated from Mother.

"Yeah, tell her Mother. How you pimped me and was

too high on your behind to get up and come see about me when

your man was molesting me and making me do unspeakable

acts. "WHERE WERE YOU?!"

Melissa had to hold me down. I had had enough of that

unstable woman. I wanted to forgive her, but she had her

nerves to come blame me for something she had created, and

never once was she concerned that I was attacked.

"Is this true, Mommy? Please tell me Claudia is

delusional from that bump on her head," Melissa said, in

astonishment.

Mother held her head in shame, and said "Yes, it's true." Melissa ran into the bathroom crying and vomiting.

"See what you've done started, Dope head!" I screamed. "Now it's all out in the open! What are you going to do about it? You can't lie and make excuses for this one!" I wanted to take back that scene so bad. I wanted my sisters to know, but not like that.

"Look, Claudia, I done apologized millions of times. There is nothing left to do," Mother cried.

"You think I want your apologies? No! Keep it! We are all concerned about Iyanna. You coming in here going crazy won't make it any better." I stated.

"Well, I'll leave, but you better find my child." She said, as she slammed the door.

"Yeah, whatever Mother. Bye!" I said, as I waved her off.

Mother speaks

After leaving Melissa's house, my heart and mind were
discombobulated. I never meant to hurt Claudia like I did. I
was sick! Why couldn't she understand that what I was fighting
was way beyond her? I knew that I was a low down dirty
shame, but there was no one that came to rescue me when my
father was molesting me. When he invited himself into my
bedroom, when I was only five years old. Yes, five years old. It
went on for years before my mother found out, and then, she
blamed me. I was kicked out of my parents' house when I was
only twelve years old, forcing me to do what I had to do.

By the time I was fifteen, my mother was serving a life
sentence for killing the FEDs. She tried reaching out to me, but
I never received her. I just couldn't get over the fact of what
my father had done to me, let alone, what my own mother had
done. My father was a disgusting pig, just like all of the men

that I let defile my little girl's body. My past hurt weighed on me like a ton of bricks. Everywhere I went, I felt the shame upon me. Never ceasing, never letting up. I prayed to God night and day. I cried out to God to wash me and renew me, but the next day comes around, and I'm itching for a sniff or a little taste. When would he hear my cry? I had suffered for too long. My burden was overbearing, and I drank my days and nights away. It felt as though there wasn't any rest for me. I had to make things right with my children before it was too late. Sometimes, I felt as though I would have been better off dead. I was just trying to be free.

***

I went into the bathroom to check on Melissa.

"Are you okay?" I asked, as I handed her a wash towel.

She looked at me with the saddest eyes that I had ever seen.

"I'm so sorry," she said, as she wiped the vomit from her mouth. "I'm sorry that I wasn't there. I always teased you about not having a father and that no one loved you when we would get into it. I'm so...sorry. I didn't know," Melissa cried.

"It wasn't your fault. How could you have known? You was a good sister. It was my battle, not yours. Thank God someone prayed for me. I don't know who, but I thank God they did. Come on, girl. I don't want to go there tonight. We have to find baby sis." I extended my hand to help her up.

"I just can't believe that she would do this to you! I want us to talk a little more about this someday. You hear me, Claudia?" Melissa said. I nodded and smiled.

"We will, we will." For the rest of the night, I took it easy. We watched movies to try and keep our minds off of the tragedy that had just took place. Iyanna was out there somewhere waiting for us to rescue her. I prayed a special prayer for her, took the strongest meds that I was given, and passed out.

The next day, the detective came by for a statement. He wanted to know if I remembered seeing anyone in the house the day Iyanna was taken, but everything was a complete blur. I mentioned the threat that Loco made concerning the money.

"But, I don't understand. He told me that I had until Thursday, or he was going to kill Iyanna," I told the detective.

"Excuse me, can I offer you anything to drink?" Melissa asked, as she walked into the dining area.

"Yes, a water, thank you."

Melissa handed the detective a bottle of water, "So, let's get back to what you were saying in reference to Loco's threat. To be completely honest with you, I think that he just wanted to throw you off," The detective stated, as he sipped on his water.

"What do you mean?" I asked, confused.

"Well, he knew that if he kidnapped someone that was close to you both," the detective said, pointing to Melissa and me, "you would be desperate enough to give them what they want." The detective was right. I couldn't believe I didn't see that coming.

"That son of!" I was so angry at myself, but how could I have known that he was going there that day? He was a slick donkey. That was for sure. I guess they got nervous when they saw me and knocked me out cold. They got me pretty good, because I don't remember seeing anyone run up on me.

Oh God come into this mix! I prayed. *I just don't know anymore. How did this even get this far?*

CHAPTER 9

The next day, the search was on. "Do you think that the cops has Iyanna's best interest at heart?" I asked Melissa, as I stared out of the bay window.

"I think so. Why do you ask that?" Melissa responded, as she took a moment from loading the dishwasher to look at me.

"Because, maybe they think that I'm just a misfit on the streets that caused all of this drama. To think about it, maybe I am," I said.

"Look, whether you hung out with the wrong crowd, or not, a life is still a life. We all have a job to do, and if anyone in the law enforcement feels that way, maybe they should look into another profession," Melissa said, as she poured herself a glass of orange juice.

I was taking that whole ordeal so hard. I was just feeling so hopeless. I emptied out my cereal, because my stomach turned with every thought of Iyanna.

"I just keep praying that I would wake up from this nightmare. I'm praying that this is all a dream," I said, as tears rolled down my face.

"Well, baby girl, I need you to wake up, because this is real, and it's about to get even realer. Let's put our game faces on. The cops are doing their job, but we need to do our part," Melissa said, as she winked at me. "Do you catch what I'm saying?"

I smiled and said, "Yeah, I got you. Let's do this." I stared into space, as I thought about the time Carrie and I was about to do a "187" on this girl that was always butting into our business. We were down for each other, ride or die. No matter what. The thought of it made me laugh. We really thought we were some gangsters. Thank God for clarity.

****

"Look, I told Yasmine that, next time she butted into our business, I was coming to look for her."

I was tired of Yasmine's games. Every time we had something going down, she was butting her big nose into our business. I couldn't stand her, and she would have to pay. Yasmine was a beautiful, uppity Latino. She thought she was more than anyone that she came in contact with. Her motto was, "Every knee shall bow at the mention of my name". I guess she thought she was Jesus. Every weekend, for three weeks, she had been coming around our block and taking all of our clients, as well as, our drug connections. She started spreading rumors and lies about Carrie and I to Sam, causing Sam to put his hands on me more frequently. I was sick of it. It *was time to show her that I wasn't the one to be played with. I*

jumped off the porch and scoped out the scene. It was 10 p.m.,

on a Wednesday night, when everyone was laying low.

"Are you sure you want to do this?" Carrie asked, as

she paced the yard back and forth.

My mind was made up. Yasmine had been bullying me

for weeks, and it was time to do something about it. It was the

night that I was going to burn her house down.

"Yes, I'm sure," I said, rubbing my hands together,

nervously.

"Alright, Ree Ree, don't be chickening out on me. I

have always been down for you," I said, while giving Carrie

the stink face.

"I'm not. That's not what I'm implying at all. I just

wanted to know if you were really game," Carrie stated,

popping her gum.

*"Yes, so, let's go," I said, signaling my finger towards
her car.*

*We jumped into Carrie's car and sped off toward
Yasmine's house. We had our gasoline and gloves ready. We
had our black ski masks to cover our faces, which we made out
of some old panty hose, and our whole attire was black all the
way to our nail polish. Yasmine's house was jammed packed
when we arrived. There were cars from the front all around to
the back. The first car that we noticed was Nino's black 1979
Chevy Nova. Nino was a part of one of the largest Latin king
gangs, a.k.a., Yasmine's baby daddy. Anytime he was around,
there was always some trouble.*

*Carrie backed into a vacant lot and shut off the lights.
We couldn't risk getting caught. My eyes stayed locked on
Yasmine's house. I was laid low in my seat with my baseball
cap merely covering my eyes. Sweat dripped down my face
with every minute that passed by. I was nervous, but I refused*

to show it. Even though we were out here to do some gangster

type stuff, we weren't crazy enough to burn it down with

anyone in it.

"Full moon tonight," Carrie said, looking up at the

dark blue sky.

"Yes, because the wolves are out," I said, pointing back

and forth between the two of us.

We laughed and continued to wait until the coast was

clear. Midnight came around, and I was woken up by a loud

noise. People shouting and fussing in front of Yasmine's house.

I rubbed the sleep out of my eyes to get a better focus. Just like

I expected, Nino was causing drama between him and his

rivals, the Sledge Hammer Gang. Yasmine ran outside,

screaming and yelling for Nino to stop and to come into the

house. Nino pushed Yasmine into the car and yelled in her face

before spitting at her.

"You monster!" Yasmine yelled, as she slapped Nino across his head.

Nino turned to slap Yasmine, but he never got the chance. His rivals started shooting and killed him and Yasmine, instantly. I held my hand up to my mouth to stop my scream from exiting. Then, I quickly shook Carrie to wake her up.

"Get up! We have to get out of here. We have to leave before anyone sees us," I said, pointing towards Yasmine's house.

Carrie quickly started the ignition, and we headed back home. The things that I had just witnessed changed my whole outlook on things. Even though I was going there to get revenge, I never wanted anyone to get hurt. Your life can be taking away from you in just seconds. The angels must have been on our side. If we would have decided to go in, and burn Yasmine's house, we would have ended up dead. Later on that night, I prayed really hard. I felt so guilty that I wished ill will *on a girl that didn't know who she was in the first place.*

Sometimes, real life had to knock you in the face, so that you

could realize how precious your life really was. God gives us

free will, but we shall suffer the consequences of our actions.

****

I didn't quite know what Melissa had on her mind to

finally end this mess, but whatever it was, I was going to make

it happen. If I was still on the streets with the same mindset, I

would have killed someone behind my family, but I found

another way to fight, and that was through Christ. I couldn't

handle it on my own. As I was praying, there was a knock at

the door, and it was Melvin.

"Mel!? What are you doing here?" I was completely

surprised. God must have heard my prayers.

"There was no way that I was going to let you go through this alone. I wasn't here the first time, and I was not going to make that mistake again." Melvin said, as he leaned in and gave me a giant hug.

Melvin was a breath of fresh air. I didn't know what it I was about that man, but he was always on time.

"It is so nice to see you, Mel. I have so much to tell you," I said, as I directed him into the kitchen. "Sit, so I can tell you all about it."

Melvin eyes kept directing towards my forehead. "You can begin with that," Melvin said, pointing at my forehead.

"They took her," I said, as I rubbed my hand across my head.

"Took who?" Melvin questioned.

"They took Iyanna. Loco and Janice." I stood and paced the floor. "They said that, if I want her back alive, I will have to come up with the hundred thousand to save her. They are

blackmailing Melissa and me," I ranted.

"Wait a minute; slow down. Melvin got up and walked

towards me to calm me down. Why is Melissa involved in this?

I'm not following," Melvin asked, as he rubbed his head in

confusion.

"Somehow, Janice knows about Melissa suing the

hospital, so she knows all about the money that she received.

Now, they have Iyanna, and I don't know what I will do!" I

screamed.

"Okay, Claudia, you have to calm down. What are the

police doing to resolve this matter?" Melvin asked, as he

guided me back to the table to take a seat. I shrugged my

shoulders.

"Everything that they possibly can, I guess," I

responded.

"Please don't do anything to get in between their job, Claudia," Melvin said, as he looked at me, squinting his eyes.

"Why are you looking at me that way?" I laughed.

"Because, I know you. I know that you are so independent and that you like taking things into your own hands."

God! I thought to myself. *He knows me too well!* I laughed, because Melvin was so right.

"Come on. Let me fix you something to eat," I said. Melvin gave one of his priceless smiles and helped me cook.

Later that day, Melissa came by the pool house.

"I got it!" Melissa yelled.

"What are you talking about, Sis?" I asked, confused.

"I will give Loco what they want. No cops; just him and I. We can't wait around too much longer. Time is running out." She said, as she sat down on the bar stool.

"Wait, wait a minute. You are talking crazy. I want Iyanna back just as bad as you do, don't get me wrong, but if we give in and give them the money, they will be winning. I want to stop them for good." I stated.

Melissa turned to me and said, "It's not about the money or if they win. It's about baby sis!"

Melvin interrupted. "She might have a point, Claudia. It is probably best just to give them what they are asking for, so that everyone can be safe." I walked up to Melissa and grabbed her by the hand.

"This is my situation, and I think I should be the one to deal with this. If it wasn't for my lifestyle, Iyanna wouldn't be caught up in this mess. I don't want you to give up your money that you, so rightfully, deserve. God is making a way right now at this very moment. We have to trust his plan. Remember, you told me to have faith. If I knew that this was what you meant by doing our "part", I would not have agreed. I'm going to fight

and not give in!"

Melissa looked at me strangely, "So, what are you

thinking?"

I bit the bottom of my lip and said, "I don't know, but I

think I want to meet up with Loco. No wires, no cops… just

him and I."

The next day came around, and it was time to set up

this meeting between Loco and I. I was determined to fight

back. I was not letting anyone control me anymore.

"Are you sure you want to do this?" Melvin asked,

worried. Melvin stayed overnight in the guestroom. He didn't

want to leave my side, so I agreed for him to stay.

"Yes, I am sure. I am the one that got everyone

involved in the first place." I responded, as I headed towards

the wash room.

"Well, just so you know, I will not be far behind."

Melvin said.

I winked at him, and said, "don't I know it!" Melvin

laughed and suggested that we pray.

He always had a way of comforting my soul. He was

God sent. After all of those years, I was finally realizing it. As

soon as Melvin and I finished praying, Melissa was knocking

on the door.

"Claudia, I don't think you should do this. I mean, I

don't know what I would do if I lose both of my sisters."

Melissa said, as she poured her a cup of coffee. I knew that

Melissa was concerned, and all, but I did not want to hear that

right now. I wanted to listen to some DMX and get pumped up.

There was no time to feel weak.

"Look, I will be okay. Try not to worry so much," I

reassured.

"I don't know, Sis, but I'll try." Melissa agreed, uncertainly.

Right when I was reaching over to grab my phone to call Loco, Sam was calling from prison. *What could Sam possibly want?* Hesitantly, I decided to answer the phone.

"Hello?" The computerized lady spoke as I answered.

"You have a collect call from Forest County Correctional Center. Will you accept the call?

"Yes." I said, as I rolled my eyes.

"Hello? Hello?" Sam said, nervously.

"Dang, Sam, can I respond!" I yelled.

"I couldn't hear you. I thought that you had declined my call," Sam replied.

"No, I'm here. What do you want?" I asked.

"Look, I think that I might have some information for you concerning your baby sis." Sam responded.

"Wait, I'm confused. How do you know about that?" I asked, as I walked outside to get a better reception.

"Just listen. That's not important. Loco has a warehouse off of 43rd Street up in Clarksville." Clarksville was a small town an hour from Nashville, Tennessee. "I think that's where they may be holding Iyanna." Sam stated.

"Okay, why are you telling me all of this? How do I know that you are not setting me up to get something out of this? How do I know if I go back there, I won't get killed?" I interrogated.

"Look, do what you want with that information. I just feel like I owe you and Carrie. I want them to suffer like I'm suffering. Being in here gives you some time to think and to really see. I just realized how blind I was. I have been praying a lot in here, and I finally feel at peace." Sam said, with authenticity in his voice.

"Okay thanks. I will look into it. Oh, and Sam…. please stay positive in and out of prison, because a lot of people say one thing behind bars until they get out. Stick with God, because he is so wonderful. I'm so glad that I found him before it was too late," I stated.

"I'm good, Claudia. You just be careful." Sam said, right before hanging up.

After hanging up with Sam, I took a minute to reflect on all of the information that was just presented to me. My head was spinning out of control. It was starting to feel like a real live movie. I made my way back into the pool house. I had to let Melvin know what was going on.

"Melvin, guess who just called my phone?" I said, as I sat on the couch next to him.

"Who?" Melvin asked, as he paused the television to direct his attention towards me.

"Sam. He told me that he has an idea where Iyanna may be," I replied.

"Sam? How would he know anything about that?" Melvin asked, with a confused look on his face.

"That's what I was thinking. He didn't say who gave him the information. All I know is that I need to find out if the information that was given is true. Thank God I got that phone call from Sam before I called Loco. That way, I will be able to break into his place and save Iyanna," I said, as I walked into the kitchen.

"Wait, Claudia, are you sure?" Melvin said, as he followed me into the kitchen. I knew that he was going to try and talk me out of it, but when my mind was made up, it was made up.

"This seems really dangerous. I cannot let you do this alone, because one thing I learned while living in the hood was to never break into someone's home. You are asking for a bullet in your behind." Melvin said, as he shook his finger at me.

"Look, I'm not crazy, Mel. I will inform the police about Loco's hideaway. I want to save baby sis and come back with her alive," I responded.

"Okay," Melvin said, while wiping his forehead, "because, you had me sweating, girl!" We looked at each other and laughed.

"Come on, boy. Let's go inform Melissa."

We met up with Melissa in her kitchen, where she was cooking the best smelling lasagna in the world! Lasagna was Iyanna's favorite dish. When we were kids and Mother wasn't drunk on her behind, she used to make that for us. Iyanna would always go back for seconds, thirds, and fourths.

"Missing baby sis, aren't you?" I asked Melissa, as I rubbed my hand across her back.

I guess my comment triggered something in Melissa, because she began to cry. "I just don't know what to do! I have one sister that's kidnapped, and the other wanting to do something very dangerous. My mother is a pimp, and my husband is a complete idiot!" Melissa screamed.

"Calm down, Melissa, It will be okay. I promise. God says when two or three are gathered in his name, he is there, so why don't we all pray. Would you like that?" I asked. Melissa wiped her eyes and nodded her head. I prayed:

"Lord, help us to trust in you and not on our flesh. We know that you see the unseen. And in Jeremiah 29:11 it says, "Your thoughts for us is peace and not evil. To give us a future and Hope. Lord, we trust that you're a man that cannot lie, so we are calling on you today to guide our steps. Cover us Lord, in Psalm 91. That we shall be covered in your precious blood. We stand in the gap of Iyanna. Keep her and protect her. In Jesus Name. Amen."

"Thank you so much, Claudia. That was beautiful and hopeful."

Melissa said, as she hugged me. "Okay, now that we all prayed. I have something that I need to tell you." I said, as I took a big bite into the lasagna.

"What is it?" Melissa asked, with one eyebrow pointing to the ceiling.

"I received a phone call from Sam today, and he gave some information to where Loco may be keeping Iyanna." Melissa almost choked on her tea.

"Wait, how would Sam even know anything about this? Is he working with Loco?" Melissa asked.

"I don't know, but he sure did sound really convincing, and I'm going to find out if it is worth the try," I stated.

"Humph, I guess so, but you're not going alone," Melissa commanded.

"That's fine. I would like for you to come, and for Mel

to stay back and watch Loco's every move." Melvin, quickly,

turned back around, as he were exiting the kitchen.

"Wait, I know you did not say what I think you said.

Tell me I am tripping?" Melvin said, furiously.

"Yes, you heard me right, Mel. Iyanna is our sister. We

have to do this, not you. Besides, we will have backup." I

responded.

"But, Claudia, we agreed that I would come." Melvin

complained like a big kid.

"Change of plans. I know you want to be there, and all,

and I really appreciate it, but trust me, it will be better this

way." Melvin nodded his head in disappointment and walked

out of the room.

"Will he be okay?" Melissa asked, concerned.

"Yeah, he will be fine. We can't concentrate on Mel

right now. We have to plan Iyanna's escape." I replied.

"We sure do. We sure do," Melissa responded, as she stared into space. "Now, come help me with these dishes." Melissa requested.

"Okay, but right after I grab another bowl!" I said, as I danced to the stove. Melissa laughed and shook her head.

"I don't know how you manage to stay so thin. Greedy tail," Melissa said, slapping me across my behind.

I laughed and said, "Favor ain't fair."

Later that night, Melissa and I went to church with Melvin.

"I'm sure glad you guys decided to show up," Sister Gloria said. Sister Gloria was a very close friend of Melvin's aunt. She invited us to come visit the church over a month ago, but we never got around to it.

"Yes, sister, I'm sure glad that we came. It is so good to see you."

She leaned in and gave us a warm hug. She gradually

pulled Melissa and me to the side. "What is going on with you

all? Someone kidnapped your baby sis?" Sister Gloria

whispered. Melissa and I looked at each other like, how does

she know this? "Look, just because I'm always at church does

not mean I don't know what's going on in the streets," Sister

Gloria added.

"Yes, ma'am. We are looking for her, and the police are,

as well," Melissa responded, as she cleared her throat.

"Just let me know if you all need anything. I am

praying for her safe return." Sister Gloria said, as she walked

away.

"What was that all about? How did she know that? It

wasn't on the news due to the severity of the threat," I rambled.

"Melvin!" Don't he know the severity of this matter?"

Melissa shouted. I, quickly, covered Melissa's mouth.

"Quiet, Melissa. We are in church. We will deal with this afterwards," I said. Thank God praise and worship was going on, because the way Melissa screamed, the whole church would have heard.

As soon as church was over, I confronted Melvin. "Melvin. Come here! I need to speak with you." I said, waving him to the back of the church, but before I could get a sentence in, Melissa bombarded her way through.

"Are you crazy?! Who gave you the right to discuss this matter with anyone? Who else have you told?" Melissa interrogated. Melissa's face turned as red as her dress she had on. Melissa was in beast mode.

"Melissa, calm down. Dang, I got this," I demanded.

"First of all, I do not know what you are talking about, and secondly, please address me as the man that I am," Melvin replied.

"Oh, really, you don't know? So, how do Sister Gloria

know about Iyanna being kidnapped?" Melissa questioned.

"I don't know. Did you ask her at all? Are did you

immediately assume that it was me that told her?" Melvin said,

as he wiped the sweat from his forehead. Melvin was

becoming uncomfortable with the accusations that Melissa was

charging him with. Every vein in his neck was visible.

"Wait a minute," I interrupted. "I am so sorry that

Melissa assumed it was you. Did you tell Sister Gloria

anything about this?" I asked, in a composed voice. If you

wanted answers, screaming and yelling was no way to get them.

"No, I did not." Melvin said, looking at Melissa.

"Okay, do you have any idea how she would know?" I

asked.

"I don't have no idea, but there she goes. We can ask

her," Melvin said, as he pointed towards Sister Gloria.

"Hey Sister! It was so nice to see you again," Melvin said, as he greeted Sister Gloria with a hug.

"Oh! Likewise, Minister Melvin. I am so proud of you and the man that you have become. God is really blessing you." Sister Gloria kissed Melvin on his cheek. Her hat was so big it covered his entire face.

"Thank you so much!" I wanted to ask you something before you leave, if you don't mind," Melvin said.

"No, no. Go right ahead," she agreed.

"You mentioned earlier that you heard something about Iyanna?" Melvin asked.

"Yes?" Sister Gloria said, as she removed her large hat that revealed her shiny gray hair.

"Could you tell us who gave you that information? I mean, if you don't mind, of course," Melvin asked.

"Well, my dear child. I was talking to one of my friends, and she said that her nephew mentioned it to her, but I thought

Death by
Association

it was quite strange that it was never shown on the news. She insisted that her nephew, Sam, do not make up stories," she replied.

"Sam?" Melissa asked.

"Yes, that's Sister Delores' nephew. By the grace of God, he has changed his whole life around, being in prison and all." Sister Gloria added, as she yawned.

"Thank you for that info, Sister, but I see that you are getting tired. We will not keep you any longer. Melvin leaned in to kiss her goodnight. Have a blessed night." Sister Gloria waved bye.

"Oh, my God! Sam was telling the truth! Someone did inform him about Loco's secret hideaway," I said, placing my hand over my mouth. It was time to get to her and get to her fast before anyone else found out!

"I am so sorry," Melissa apologized to Melvin, while pouting her lips.

Kathleen D.
Richardson

0202

"Don't worry about it. I know that you are crazy!" Melvin said, jokingly.

"Ha-ha!" Melissa mocked him.

"Look guys. Time is running out, and if we go to the police about this, they will make it worst for Iyanna. If Loco knows that we know where he is hiding, he will take Iyanna far away and maybe even kill her. We have to be smart and fast." We all agreed and decided that tomorrow would be our day.

Around 2 a.m., I was woken up to Melissa and Gary yelling outside by the pool. I walked by the front door so that I could get a better listen.

"Look Gary, I don't want you here, okay?! I can do bad all by myself!" Melissa shouted.

"I know baby." Gary lowered his tone. "All I am saying is to give me another chance. Yes, I messed up, but that was when you were working all the time and when you were never home. Some nights, you barely wanted to make love anymore.

I tried talking to you about it, put you just pushed my feelings

aside. My ego was bruised, and she placed a temporary

bandage on it. I'm sorry," Gary pleaded.

"Look, don't blame this on me! There were times when

you wasn't there, either, and I never betrayed you that way. To

top it off, you shared something that was so private. This whole

mess is your fault," Melissa said, as she splashed water from

the pool into Gary's face. Gary wiped the water from his eyes.

"I don't know what I was thinking. With the help of

God, we can make it," Gary said, as tears rolled from his eyes.

"I don't know, Gary. God will have to really clean my

heart, or even, give me a new one to forgive you, but for now,

until all of this blows over, I think that you should stay away

and respect my wishes." Gary placed his hands in the air and

gave up his fight.

I walked outside to where Melissa was slumped over

with her head between her legs balling her eyes out.

"Melissa what's the matter?" I asked, as though I never heard a single word.

"Gary came by begging to return, but how can we ever come back from this? Every time I look at him now, all I see is rage. He is the cause of all of this! This is such a nightmare!" Melissa cried.

"I know, I know." I comforted her, as I wiped her tears. "When someone that you love and trust with your life betrays you in an unimaginable way, you just don't know what to do. It is like there is no sunshine from all of the rain, but after all of the rain, hail, sleet and snow, the sun will surely shine again. Just shelter yourself with the love of God. I've been where you're at. I've been let down, beat down etc., but I made it. I learned to fight, no matter the circumstances. I still struggle, but now I know that I don't have to struggle alone. It will be okay. We will take it one day at a time."

Melissa wipes her face. "Sorry we woke you up. Come stay with me tonight. I don't want to be alone."

"Sure," I agreed. "No problem."

The next morning, I woke up to something smelling fantastic in the kitchen.

"I guess Sissy is feeling better!" I said, as I jumped out of the bed, but to my surprise it was my mother. *God! She is always around!* I thought to myself.

"Good morning, Daughter," She said, as she continued to stir the grits.

"Good morning," I mumbled.

"Where is the sunshine this morning?" She asked, sarcastically.

I was not about to entertain her shenanigans that morning. I just continued to sip my coffee and read the paper. Even though that breakfast was smelling so good, I was still holding a grudge from the other day.

"Look, I know I said this a million times, but I am sorry about the other day. I know you love your sister too much to let anything happen to her intentionally," Mother stated, as she positioned a plate of food in front of me. I guess this was her way of clearing the air.

"I'm good. I forgot all about that," I lied, as I pushed the plate away.

She looked at me for, at least, two minutes without saying a word and walked away. I guess she didn't know what to do or say anymore.

"So, are we all set?" Melissa asked, as she hopped down the stairs.

"Yes. Melvin is hiding out by Loco's homeboy's house. He will call us as soon as he sees Loco," I responded.

Loco never missed a beat from visiting Brick, so we knew that he would show up sooner or later. Melissa took a couple months off from work, so she was able to move around freely.

"Does anyone want to let me know what's going on?" Mother asked.

"No. Nothing that you need to worry about." I said, as I rolled my eyes. We still didn't trust her, because if she wanted a hit bad enough, she would do and say whatever she needed just to get high. We couldn't risk anyone finding out about our plan.

"Well, whatever it is, be careful." Mother said, as she walked outside to smoke.

"Girl, I am some nervous. I hope all goes as planned." I said, as I tightened up my J's.

"Me, too, girl. God, when will he call?" Melissa said, impatiently, as she stared at her phone.

"Be patient, he will," I said.

Melissa and I were dressed in all black. Black tights, black hoodies, and our black Jordan's. She also suggested that we wore extra clothing underneath as a disguise to make us look bigger just in case someone saw us. We could not risk being seen. Three o'clock came, and the phone was ringing. It was Melvin. He was such a sport for camping out by Brick's.

"Hey, so here is the deal. Loco just arrived at Bricks' so get going, now!" Melvin demanded.

We, immediately, grabbed the car keys and was pushing it about 120 mph down the interstate. We had no time to waste, because it was definitely of the essence, but it seemed as though Melissa was pushing it a little too fast.

"Slow down a bit, Melissa. We don't need a cop stopping us and possibly spoiling our plans," I demanded.

Melissa flashed her badge at me, "Girl, I got this! Did you forget that I am the FED? We gave each other a high five and laughed.

"Well, proceed!" I shouted.

Forty-five minutes later, we arrived at our destination.
We slowly approached the abandoned looking warehouse that
was surrounded by a bunch of scary looking trees. Loco had
about five pit bulls; two in the front, and three in the back, but
we came prepared. Melissa managed to grab a few things from
work. We had stun guns, and yes, a couple of real guns. Yes,
Jesus was my Lord and Savior, but I had to be ready for
whatever.

"Girl, let's pray before we go in here. I am so nervous!"
I suggested. After Melissa and I prayed, we were ready for war.

"Let's go," Melissa, said as she jumped out of the car.
The place was extremely junky and stinky. It was an old
abandoned building with lots of tracker tires on the outside,
and it smelled like old dog poop. It seemed as though we
arrived at the right time, because no one was insight. Hopefully,

Iyanna was here. As for the dogs, we had to shoot them with

the stun guns, because they just wouldn't shut up.

"Iyanna, are you here?" I asked, in a whispery voice, as

I paced my way down the dark hall, giving me a moment of

Déjà vu. My skin began to crawl.

"Claudia! In here!" Melissa called out. As I entered the

tiny room, there Iyanna was, half-naked, beaten, Tied and

gagged.

"Oh, my God!" I cried. "Iyanna!"

"Hurry up and untie her!" Melissa screamed.

As I started to untie Iyanna's arms and legs, my phone

vibrates, and it was Melvin.

"Where were you? I been calling for over twenty

minutes now!

"Get out of there, now! Loco and his boy left about

twenty minutes ago in a hurry! I think they may know

something!" Melvin stated, nervously.

"But, how?" I asked.

"I don't know! Just go!" He commanded. After hanging

up with Melvin, I took a moment to scan the room. And there it

was, a red light. We were being recorded the whole time.

"Come on, Sis! We got to go!" I yelled.

We hurried up and untied Iyanna and ran outside.

Thankfully, the dogs were still weak. I hurried and put Iyanna's

fragile body in the car, and we dashed off. We decided to take

the opposite direction home. We had to make it to the nearest

hospital, fast.

CHAPTER 10

Not too far down the road, we were being chased! It was Loco! They must have known a shortcut.

"Oh, my God, Melissa, drive faster!" I screamed.

"I'm going as fast as I can!" She yelled. I, quickly, grabbed my phone to call the police. As I was on the phone with the police, I looked around in search of any type of street signs to direct them to us.

Boom! Boom! Boom!

"Arrrgh!" We all screamed at once, because they were shooting at us.

"Grab my gun, now!" Melissa ordered. I had no choice but to defend us. It was either us or them, so I pulled back the trigger and released fire. I directed the gun at their tires, causing them to have a blowout. Melissa managed to turn off on a street directing us to the nearest hospital. We had finally lost them.

A few minutes later, we arrived at the hospital.

"Oh, God, we are so happy that we found you, Iyanna. I am so sorry!" I cried.

All Iyanna could do was cry. She was so relieved that she was safe. We had a million and one questions, but we didn't want to pressure her. She had been through enough.

"I am so angry!" I screamed.

"I want them dead. I hate the ground that they walk on for doing this to baby sis!" I said, as I paced the hospital floor. I had to calm myself down and remember my choice of words. I walked away to have some alone time to pray. I couldn't stop thinking about the horrible things that I had been through in my life. How could anyone endure this type of living?

"God, please allow your holy angels to watch over my baby sis. Continue to guide me into the right direction and the right people," I prayed, as I paced the hall, back and forth.

Meanwhile, the police were on their way to search for Loco. "I hope they find them. They had the nerves to shoot at

us! I'm so mad! They deserve everything that's coming to
them!" Melissa shouted, angrily.

About thirty minutes after arriving at the hospital,
Mother rushed in.

"Where is my baby?" She cried. The last time I seen
Mother run that fast was when she was getting her behind
beaten by one of her men.

"She's in the back with the doctor. We can't go back
there right now," I said.

"I am just so happy she is safe. Thank you, God!"
Mother stated. Every time she showed concern for my sisters, it
brought back too many bad memories, so I just walked away
from her without saying another word.

An hour later, Melvin arrived at the hospital, and I was
so relieved to see him.

"Thank God, you made it," I said, as I ran to him.

"Is she okay?" Melvin asked.

"She is doing fine. She's in the back with the doctor right now. I replied.

"How about you? Are you fine?" Melvin asked, with a frown on his face.

"Well, you know me… strongest of them all; I have to be fine." I said, with sarcasm.

"Come here, Claudia." Melvin pulled me into him. "Look, I am so fed up with you and this "I'm okay when I'm not" attitude. It's time to allow yourself to be vulnerable. It's good for the soul."

I tried to hold myself together, but all I could do was cry. I had had about enough of all of that madness that was going on in my life. I just couldn't deal with it anymore.

"Let it all out. It's time to set yourself free. Humble yourself. Let it all go," Melvin said, as he rubbed my head gently. I must admit, it felt darn good just to release everything that I had been holding inside for the past few weeks.

"I'm just so glad that she is alive and well, but I will be more relieved when Loco and Janice are behind bars once and for all. I said, as I wiped my tears.

"I know, my love. I know!" Melvin replied.

A few hours later, we heard Melissa screaming, but we couldn't make out what she was saying.

"What?! What is the matter, Melissa?" I asked in concern.

"They got them!" Melissa cried.

"Wait, did they find Loco and Brick?" I asked apprehensive.

"Yes! They got them. It's over, Claudia. You can finally be free! We can all be free!" Melissa hugged me tightly. All I could do was cry my eyes out. What I had been praying for had finally come to past. *Thank you, Lord!*

"Where did they find them?" I asked. Melissa explained to us how they were caught walking by a nearby gas station not too far from Loco's warehouse. "I guess they did not have a

spare tire!" Melissa laughed.

"They got Loco and Brick, but they haven't found

Janice, yet. They put out a warrant for her arrest, so hopefully,

they find her soon. Let's go break the news to Iyanna."

Melissa grabbed my hand, as we ran down the hall to

baby sis's room. Melissa walked into Iyanna's room dancing.

She picked up a rose from the vase that Iyanna had by her

bedside, sniffed it, and twirled. Iyanna looked at me with a grin

on her face.

"What's wrong with your sister?" Iyanna asked, weakly.

"Girl, guess what?" Melissa said, still dancing. Iyanna

nodded her head.

"They caught Loco and "Chubby," I shouted, before

Melissa could say anything. I was so happy and relieved that

those two guys were off the streets. Iyanna was relieved, as we told her the awesome news. All we wanted to do was go home

and get back to our lives.

Later on that night, I decided to go by Iyanna's house to

pick up a few things that she needed. Of course, Melvin made

sure to come with me. He had been acting more like a

bodyguard than anything else. To tell you the truth, it wasn't

half bad to allow someone in and slowly let that wall fall. Upon

approaching Iyanna's house, Mrs. Carol, Iyanna's neighbor,

was standing on her porch looking towards the back yard of

Iyanna's house.

"Hey, Mrs. Carol," I waved. "Is everything okay?" She

shook her head, as she walked towards our way.

"They had someone in your sister's house." She said,

pointing her finger at the house. I turned to look at Melvin, and

my heart dropped to my knees. Just when I thought everything

was over, but how could it be with Janice still out there

somewhere?

"So, you actually seen someone in her house?" I asked, curiously.

Mrs. Carol nodded, again, "Yes, I seen two people. Look like a woman and a man. I tried to get a better look, but as soon as I went back into my house to get my glasses, they were gone," she said, shaking her head. "I don't know what the world is coming to. I tell you these kids these days is ruining everything for the good, the old and the young. But, my dear heavenly father is watching everything. Mm hmm. Oh yes He is!" Mrs. Carol started to preach and shout.

"Okay, Mrs. Carol," I said, as I touched her arm to calm her down. "I'm all with praising the Lord and everything, but I need to know a little more about what you have seen tonight," I said.

"Oh, yes, baby. Thank you, Jesus!" She said, as she wiped the sweat from her face. "Let me get back on track. It's just that, when the Holy Spirit is on you, it's hard to stay still."

Melvin had his eyes closed as though he was praying, as well.

"Yes, Mrs. Carol, I know what you mean," Melvin added with his hands folded. I elbowed Melvin in his stomach, because I knew how Mrs. Carol was. It didn't take much to get her started again. I needed details, and I needed them now.

"All I know is that they pulled off in a red pickup truck. One of the newer ones," she said, with her arms folded.

"Okay, Mrs. Carol, thanks a lot. You go back in. It's not safe at this time of night," I said, as I walked her up her steps.

"You be careful, child. God bless you," she said, as she closed her door. I walked back to my car, popped the trunk, and grabbed my iron bat.

"Protection," I said, as I waved the bat in the air. Melvin grabbed the bat out of my hand.

"I'll hold that." He was becoming a bit annoying. I stuck the key in the door and turned slowly as my heart pounded away. The door squeaked, as I opened it, making me stop in my tracks.

"Shh," Melvin said.

"I'm trying," I whispered. We slowly walked inside the house, making sure that we were ready if anyone came at us. I, quickly, reached for the lamp that was on side of her love seat. Melvin signaled that he was going to walk down the hallway and for me to stay put. I nodded my head and mouthed for him to be careful. As Melvin walked down the hall, I scoped out the kitchen, grabbing the largest knife that I could find. I peeked inside of the kitchen closet with my knife in my hand. Nothing... no one, so I walked back into the living room and saw a shadow on the porch. I walked to the window to get a better view. As I was slowly opening the blinds, I felt a warm touch on the back of my neck. I jumped and attacked, stabbing

Melvin in his arm twice.

"Oh, God!" I screamed in terror, dropping the knife

onto the floor. I became sick as I saw the blood leaking out of

Melvin's arm. Melvin's face was scrunched up in pain, as tears

filled his eyes.

"I'm so sorry, Melvin. I didn't know."

I grabbed Iyanna's throw blanket off of her recliner,

wrapped it around his arm, and quickly tied it into a knot.

Melvin groaned in pain, as I hurried and swung the door open,

completely forgetting about the shadow that I saw earlier. I

struggled my way down the steps, placing Melvin's manly

body into the car. I ran on the driver side and took off back to

the hospital.

"I know I was being overprotective, but did you have to

go ahead and cut me?" Melvin laughed and grunted at the same

time. I didn't find anything amusing about that incident. I

began to cry, hysterically, as I thought back to the day my

mother stabbed Joe. Joe was the only man that did not try

anything with me. He was a good man until mother got a hold

to him. I often had nightmares of that horrific night and

wondered whatever happened to him.

"It's okay, Claudia. It was a mistake. It could have been

worst," Melvin said, as he tried reaching over to comfort me,

but his pain stopped him in his tracks.

"I know, but what if I would have killed you. Your

young life would have been over, as well as mines," I said,

wiping my nose. I couldn't make it to the hospital fast enough.

I was two minutes away, in which it felt like an eternity.

I made sure that I pulled up to the main entrance,

because I needed help with Melvin, because he was slim, but

heavy.

"Someone please help!" I yelled out at the nurses sitting

at the nurse's station.

"What happened?" Melissa asked, as she ran towards the car. I began to cry.

"Mrs. Carol said someone was in the house. We got the bat out the car, Melvin went down the hallway, I grabbed the knife, someone was outside, and… and," I started hyperventilating.

"Wait, wait, calm down," Melissa said, grabbing me and walking me to a nearby chair in the lobby. The nurses had already put Melvin on a stretcher and had taken him to the ER.

"Here, drink this." Melissa handed me a cup of water, which went straight down my chin from the way my teeth were chattering. "Okay, you need to slow down, and tell me what happened. Why is Melvin full of blood?" Melissa looked down at my hands. "As well as you?"

Before I could calm myself down and explain what had happened, a police officer was walking our way.

"Excuse me, ma'am, but I have a few questions that I need you to answer for me." He flipped open his notepad, as he studied me from bottom to top.

"Is that your blood or Mr. Woodman's?" He asked.

"Melvin's... Mr. Woodman's," I stuttered.

I looked over at Melissa and swallowed hard. I wanted her to jump in and save me like she used to when we were kids. When one of the neighborhood kids wanted to fight me, Melissa would step in and rock their world. The kids used to tease Melissa, *"Light skin don't win, you mutt,"* they would yell, but after Melissa got finish placing her Italian hands on them, they wouldn't say nothing else. Every time my sister was home, I thought I was big stuff.

"Claudia?" Melissa tapped me on my thigh, bringing my attention back.

"What happened tonight? How did Mr. Woodman get the knife wounds in his left arm?" He interrogated. Even

though I knew I was innocent, my guilt made me feel otherwise.
I took a deep breath, straightened up my posture, and told the
officer exactly what had happened.

"Well, Ms. James, that's exactly how Mr. Woodman's
story went, so you are in the clear," he said, as he took a seat
next to me. "But, I am a bit concerned about the intruder that
Iyanna's neighbor…" *He licks his finger and turns the page in
his notepad,* "Mrs. Carol, saw a little earlier tonight. Would
you happen to know of anyone that could have went to your
sister's house?" I shook my head no.

"Not really. Maybe, it was Janice. They are still looking
for her in the case of her kidnapping, but I'm not a hundred
percent sure." As he was questioning me, all I could think
about was poor Melvin and what I accidently did to him, or,
did I? Maybe it was in my bloodline to kill just like my
grandmother did. I shook the thoughts out of my head.

"Sir, if you don't mind, I would like to have a minute alone in the chapel. I'm dealing with a lot of unresolved issues right about now, and I'm not thinking straight. I loss a friend, I rescued my baby sister from her kidnapper, I was shot at, and I stabbed my best friend, so please, if you don't mind, I would like to be left alone. Please." I bent forward and buried my face into my hands.

Melissa rubbed me on my back, while telling the officer thank you and to give me a second. He agreed and walked away.

"I'll be back," I told Melissa, as I wiped my tears.

I grabbed my purse and walked towards the restroom. I turned on the faucet and splashed water in my face a couple of times, forgetting that my hands were covered in Melvin's blood. I smeared blood all over my face, then I cried at the sight of the blood.

"God, what is happening to me? Just when I thought I had it all together."

I washed my hands and made my way to the chapel. There were two old couples, and a young girl close to my age that sat there weeping. *Her burden couldn't be as bad as mine.* I thought selfishly to myself. I kneeled down and started to pray to God to remove all of my burdens and the curses from upon me. I prayed the prayer of Jabez and meditated on his word. After thirty minutes of praying, I felt more at peace. Before leaving, I noticed the young girl was still weeping, uncontrollably. I walked up to her and asked if she would like for me to pray with her. Her face lit up with joy. She told me how her parents left her when she was only two years old and that, ever since, she has been bouncing from foster home to foster home. She couldn't understand why God never loved her enough to give her a stable home.

"I'm sorry that you went through that, but you are not alone. Never, for a second, should you allow yourself to believe God isn't with you."

I talked to her for hours, before I had realized the time that had passed by. I had to check on Melvin. She thanked me for my sincere words, we exchanged numbers, and said goodbye. I truly believed that God had put me in that situation for that particular reason. God is so mysterious; his wisdom is far beyond our understanding. Melvin was out of surgery, and he was placed in recovery in Room 202.

"Hello," I said, as I slowly walked into his room. Melvin was lying there with a sling around his arms and his eyes close. I kissed him on his forehead and whispered that I was sorry.

"God told me to tell you, enough already," Melvin chuckled. I laughed, as I placed his get well balloons and card on the stand next to his bed.

Kathleen D. Richardson   0230

"Did they ever find out who was at Iyanna's house?" Melvin questioned, clearing his throat.

"No, the police went to her room and asked her a few questions, but I haven't heard anything, yet. "But, how are you doing?" I asked, with my lip poked out, as I sat at the foot of his bed.

"All I know is that I will announce myself before entering any room that you're in." We began to laugh at once.

I sat in his room for the remainder of the night. I walked into Iyanna's room every now and then just to make sure that she was okay. Two people were in the hospital because of me and the people I knew. I needed God to show up more than ever before.

Chapter 11

The next morning, Melvin was released from the

hospital, and I drove him back to Melissa's, so that he could

rest. I jumped into the shower, because I was looking and

smelling a mess. After twenty minutes of relaxing in the

shower, I was ready to run some errands for the day. I threw on

my black sun dress and my silver flip-flops, freshened up my

curls, and I was good to go. I left Melvin a note on the night

stand to let him know that I would be gone for a couple of

hours, and that, if he needed anything to ring my cell. I made

sure to turn on the alarm and lock the door.

I jumped into my Honda Civic and headed towards the

store. After shopping for, at least, an hour, because Iyanna

called with a list of things that she needed, I received a blocked

call.

"Hello?" I answered. No one said anything. Only

breathing sounds came through the receiver.

"Hello?" I asked, again. Silence. I rolled my eyes and

placed my phone inside the cup holder. As soon as I drove off,

my phone rang again, this time someone spoke.

"You think this is over? Nah, it isn't over. Not until I

have your head; including your man's." My throat became dry

and fear shook my whole entire body.

"Who, who is this?" I asked, fearfully. The voice that

came from the receiver was a robotic sound as though someone

was disguising their voice.

"You will find out sooner than later." The sound of the

dial tone made my heart tremble. I drove as fast as I could back

to the house to check on Melvin. Fear rushed through my bones,

as I thought about the day Iyanna was taken.

"Oh, God. This can't be happening, again." But, it was.

When I got into the house, Melvin was gone. The alarm was

unset and stuff was all over the place. The table lamp was on

the floor, and the curtains from the bay window were torn.

Signs of struggle was everywhere. My world started spinning,

and my mind began racing. The thought of Melvin possibly

being hurt made me fall to my knees. This can't be happening,
again.

"No, no, no!" I screamed, as I began knocking things
off of the walls. "Why Lord? Why is my life so hard?" I
grabbed my phone and dialed Melissa.

"Hello," she answered.

"They took him, they took him," I cried into the phone.

"Took who?" She asked, confused.

"Melvin," I cried. "I left Melvin alone while I went to
grab a few things from the store, and I received an anonymous
phone call while I was out. They said that they were going to
kill me and my man," I explained, as I walked outside to catch
my breath.

"Where are you? Did you call the cops?" Melissa asked.

"No, I didn't, and I'm to your house," I replied.

"I will call them, and I'm on my way," Melissa said, before hanging up.

I, quickly, went back into the pool house and locked the door. I grabbed my iron bat and sat right by the window. I tried calling Melvin phone a few times, but it went straight to voicemail.

"God, please help your faithful servant. It's because of me that your servant is in trouble. His work for you here is not complete. Please Lord, send your angels now. In Jesus Name, Amen." I made my sign of the cross and continued to wait on Melissa.

Twenty minutes later, Melissa arrived with the police. I was so sick and tired of the police in my life. I was so desperate for my life to be normal, but then again, I never knew what normal felt like.

"Hey," Melissa said, as she ran towards me.

"I don't know how they got in here. I set the alarm and everything," I explained to the cops.

"Does anyone else besides your immediate family know the code to the security alarm? Including Mr. Woodman?" The officer asked Melissa, as him and his partner dusted for fingerprints.

"Yes, Melvin knows the code, but what that have to do with anything?" I asked, aggravated. Melissa pushed me aside, giving me that, "*I got this*" look.

"No, just us…. and my mother," She said, rubbing her eyes. "No, she wouldn't, would she?" I said, pacing back and forth. Melissa turned to the officer and gave them a picture of our mother.

"She has been M.I.A from the hospital since yesterday. She is not working right now, highly addicted to drugs, and she would do anything for a hit." As I thought back, she had been hanging around Melissa's house lately. She made me believe that she missed being home so that she could leave the facility

and come live at Melissa's. This could have been her plan all

along.

"Okay, we will get on it, ASAP. Meanwhile, you guys

stay put in a safe place. I will have an officer guarding your

sister's hospital room 24/7 until we get this mystery solved,"

He nodded his head and got into his vehicle.

My thoughts started running wild, as the tears fell from

my face. If this was my mother's doing, what type of person

was she really? I grabbed my phone and my purse, and headed

out the door.

"Where are you going?" Melissa followed me towards

the door.

"I can't stay here," I said, as I walked outside. Staying

in that house made me crazy. I had to move around before I

lost it.

"Well, the officer insisted for us to stay here, and to tell you the truth, I'm sick and tired of your mess," Melissa said, standing in the doorway with her arms folded. I turned to Melissa and walked up to her slowly. I stared at her for a moment, as though, I did not recognize the person that was standing right in front of me. The person that I grew up with.

"I'm sorry that you feel that way. Your services are no longer needed," I threw my purse around my shoulder, jumped in my car, and smashed off. I heard Melissa yelling out to me as I left, but I ignored her plea.

"It's just you and me, now, God," I stated, as a tear rolled down my cheek.

I decided to stay out at a nearby hotel. Once I checked in, I tried calling Melvin's phone once again and, that time, someone answered, but it wasn't Melvin.

"All you had to do was hand over the money, but instead you and your sister wanted to play super hero. You took away my man, now, I'm about to take away yours. If you

don't give us what we asked for by tomorrow, he will be

hanging from the fifth floor of the Marriot where you are

staying." I jumped off the bed and looked out the window. My

eyes scanned the parking lot from left to right.

"Janice, I know this is you. Are you working with my

mother? You better not lay a hand on Melvin!" I yelled through

the receiver.

Before I could say another word, Janice yelled, "Have

the money by tomorrow, or else!"

I hurried and threw my things back into my duffle bag,

grabbed the hotel key off of the nightstand, and exited the room.

It wasn't safe here; it wasn't safe anywhere.

"Is everything okay with the room? I can get you a new

one," the tall, dark-skinned woman from behind the desk asked,

as she looked at the computer screen.

"Oh no, ma'am. That won't be necessary. Something important came up, and I need to check out," I replied, looking around the lobby. I was so paranoid, and it showed.

"Okay, very well. Is everything alright?" She probed.

"No, I'm fine. Here is the key," I handed her the key, signed the proper documents, and fled the scene.

Times like that, I wished that I could go and hide away at my mother's or grandma's house, like normal people, but I had neither. I cried, as I thought about how lonely I felt. I pulled over on the side of the road to collect myself. It was raining outside, and my tears weren't making it no better. As I sat in my car, I reflected back on how helpful Melvin had been through all of that. If it wasn't for him, I would still be lost. I reached inside of my purse and grabbed my phone, opened up my bible app to Psalm 91, and read the last chapter, and it was perfect for that night.

While reading my bible, a text from Melissa came

through.

Melissa: Where are you? Mother showed up to the

house all high, so I guess that rules her out. Please call me.

I rolled my eyes, finished my scripture, started my car,

and headed back to Melissa's. I took a deep breath before

exiting the car, as I stared at the living room light that was still

on.

"I was hoping everyone would have been sleep by

now," I said, gazing at the time.

It was only 8:30, but it felt close to midnight, because

the night had really been moving fast. Before I could step out

of the car, Melissa was racing over to me.

"Oh, I'm so happy to see you," she said, hugging my

neck. I didn't respond, as I pressed the alarm button on my

keys to lock my car. "Come on," she said, grabbing my hand.

"There is someone that I want you to meet." I rolled my eyes in

annoyance and wondered who this could possibly be.

As we entered into the house, I could see a tall, brown-

skinned, slender man standing by the dining room table with a

book in his hand.

"Hello, you must be Claudia," he said, extending his

hand. I gave a slight grin, as I shook his hand.

"This here is Bishop George Cunningham. He is Gary's

and my pastor at Holy Ghost Baptist Church. He came by to

speak to Gary and me about our problems, and I thought it

would be a good idea for you to speak to him, as well," Melissa

said, as she guided me to the sofa. I looked around for my high

mother, but she was nowhere to be found.

"Where is Mother?" I asked Melissa. Melissa pointed

towards the back room.

"She is sleeping." Pastor George placed his bible on the table next to me.

"Do you know the Lord, Ms. Claudia?" He said, as he folded his hands in his lap.

"Yes sir, I do," I said, as I placed my phone on the sofa next to me. "I've just recently rededicated my life to him, but it seems as though ever since I decided to do that, things just keep on happening back-to-back. Not good things, either. I mean, I know your faith has to be tested, but some things can really kill your faith, as well. Sometimes, I just don't understand," I said, as I sat back on the sofa and bit down on my lip.

"Mm, I see," he said, placing his hand on his chin. "When things are coming at you like a wave, that's when you have to stand and believe on God's word more than ever before. The things we see can really have us questioning our faith, but God wants to see if you will still believe, no matter what your eyes may see, believe it, or not. The things that you face are

only steps to bring you to your destiny; your resting place. You

see, your trials and your tribulations build your staircase to get

you to God's glory. Keep on praying and trusting and always

stay hopeful, because it's not about you. Everything is for His

glory." He opened up his bible and pointed out a few bible

verse for me to meditate on.

"How is it going?" Melissa asked, placing two bottles

of apple juice on the table.

"Very good," I said smiling. Even though my good

friend was out there somewhere, I could still feel God's peace

resting upon me. Bishop spent another thirty minutes talking

and praying before he left. He also blessed Melissa's home.

"I can't wait to see you in church on Sunday, Claudia. I

will be praying for a safe return for Melvin," he said, before

closing the door behind him. That was just what I needed.

Chapter 12

The sun was shining, and the birds were chirping, but

deep in my heart, it was only darkness and sadness, as I

thought about poor Mel. It had been two days since he had

been missing. I reached over, grabbed my bible off of the

nightstand, turned to Galatians 6, and said a prayer for Melvin.

It was the day that Iyanna got out of the hospital. That was the

only thing that was good in my life at that moment. I reached

over to grab my phone to dial Melvin's number again, but my

mother walked into the room interrupting me.

"Hey. Can I speak to you about some things?" She

asked, standing at the door.

"About what?" I asked, still looking down at my phone.

She walked inside the room and gently closed the door.

"It's about Melvin," she whispered, as she sat down on

the bed. I sat up and placed my phone on the night stand.

"What about him? Did you have anything to do with his

kidnapping?" I said, with my nostrils flared, as my breathing

became rapid. The next few seconds between my question and

her answer felt like hours. She got up from the bed and walked

towards the window.

"You know how I've been dealing with an addiction all
of my life and placing it before anyone that I love?" She
cleared her throat and backed herself into the corner. She
placed her head down and folded her hands together. Tears ran
down her face, as she forced her words to exit from her lips.
"One night, as I was itching for a hit, I came across Janice."
My heart began to race, as I placed my feet on the floor. "That
was the night that I left you and Melissa. The night that she
found out that I pimped you. I was so depressed and didn't
know what else to do," she said, crying profusely.

"So, what are you saying, Mother?!" I said, raising my
voice, as I balled up my fist. I knew that the bible said to honor
thy mother and thy father, whoever he was, but today was
going to be the day that I was going to break that law. Mother
placed her hands in the air.

"Wait, wait, let me finish. I made a deal that if she
would give me a hit and let me know where Iyanna was that I

would give her the security code to Melissa's home. And that way, she could get what she wanted, so she agreed. I wrote down the security code and took the crack. She began walking away before she told me where Iyanna was. I yelled for her to let me know, but she never told me. I'm so tired of messing up, Claudia. I'm just so tired," she said, crying into her shirt.

I closed my eyes and took a deep breath. Tears fell from my eyes, and fire filled my veins. My throat became tight, holding back my words. I couldn't believe that she sold her own daughter out for a quick hit. But, then again, she did give me a childhood from hell. She was sick, weak, and unable to control herself. She was a deceived creature that really didn't know any better.

"Okay," I calmed myself down. "Was Janice with anyone that night you saw her?" She picked herself up from the floor and carefully walked my way.

"There was this guy. Short, medium-built, dark-skinned guy. She called him Taz. They drove off in a newer model red truck," she said, wiping her face. I grabbed my phone and logged onto Facebook. I typed in Janice and looked through her friends for anyone named Taz. I did not see anyone named Taz, but I did come across someone like my mother described.

"Is this him?" I asked, showing her the picture.

"Yes," she replied, pointing her finger at the phone. "That's him alright." I shook my head.

"Okay, good, good. This gives us a lot to go on. Thank you for being honest," I said, as I looked around in my closet for something to wear. Mother smiled and left the room.

"Melissa!" I yelled from the bathroom.

"What is all the yelling about?" Melissa asked, mean-mugging me. "You know I can't stand yelling." I looked at her up and down.

"I guess not, after all the yelling you and Gary did. We laughed at once. "Anyways, what is it?" Melissa asked, leaning on the bathroom door.

"Momma came in my room this morning and confessed to giving Janice the security code to your house." Melissa eyes widened.

"Say what?" I grabbed her arm.

"Wait, before you start focusing on her, she did give me some vital information that we need to give to the police in order for them to possibly locate Melvin. Janice was with a guy they called Taz. He is Janice's friend on Facebook," I said, showing her the picture on Facebook.

"Ooh, that's Sharon's son! His name is Christopher. I can't believe this. He is only sixteen years old. How did he get caught up with someone like Janice? His mother did not raise him this way," Melissa said, shaking her head at the phone.

"Well, no matter how you were raised, when the streets hit you, it hits you," I stated.

"Well, I'm going to go have a talk with his mother today after we pick up Sis from the hospital.

I nodded my head, "Sounds good."

That was just like Janice to seduce a man and put him under her manipulative spell. I didn't know what is was about her, but every man that she was with did exactly what she told them to do, and it always ended badly for them. Some say that she knew voodoo. Who knew? Maybe, that's why I'm going through all of this hell. Melissa avoided mother as much as possible for the remainder of the day. Two o'clock came, and it was time to go and get Iyanna from the hospital.

"Come on, let's go!" Melissa yelled from the garage.

"Yawl going pick up Iyanna from the hospital?" Mother asked, as she entered into the living area.

"Mm-hmm," I said grabbing my phone off of the coffee table. She stood there, with her arms folded, looking out of the window. I paused from what I was doing and cut my eye at her. "Is something the matter?" I asked, out of curiosity.

She chuckled. "No, no. I was just thinking that it had been so long since we've all been underneath the same roof. I guess God does hear a sinner's prayer." She walked into the kitchen and grabbed her coffee mug.

"Well, just don't touch anything while we're gone. You have caused enough of trouble as it is," I said, before closing the garage door.

"What was that all about?" Melissa turned to ask me.

"What? Her? Nothing important. Trust me," I said, as I buckled my seatbelt. As we were pulling out of the garage, I noticed something, black and shiny, slumped over in Melissa's landscape.

"What is that?" I pointed at the flower bush. Melissa

squinted her eyes.

"I don't know, but I'm going to find out." Melissa

threw the car in park, and we got out of the car to get a better

look. The closer we got, the clearer it became. Melissa pulled

back the shiny material just enough to reveal what changed my

life. I screamed at the top of my lungs. I screamed so loud that

the neighbor's car alarm went off. It was Melvin's body.

"They killed him!" I wailed.

My mother came rushing out of the house. Rage and

anger rushed over me, as I saw her standing there as though she

was sad. I ran up to her and pulled her down by her hair. My

fist met her face several times, until there was blood drawn.

"This is all your fault. This is all your fault!" I cried.

Melissa pulled me off of her, causing her and me to fall

to the ground. All of the neighbors were outside, talking and

watching. Melissa stayed in a predominantly white

neighborhood, so I guess it was something that they had only

seen in their wildest dreams. I couldn't blame them, though.

The horrific sight would make anyone stare. Less than fifteen

minutes later, the ambulance and the cops were there, once

again.

I couldn't stop myself from crying uncontrollably. I felt

helpless and defeated. It felt like my body was going to take

over itself and do something that I would probably later regret.

I'm not proud of the way I came at my mother, but she had it

coming a long time now. She sat there, with her hands over her

nose, as the tears race down her face. An evil grin was

plastered across my face, as I thought about everything that she

put me through. The only man, who had ever shown me what

love was, was now dead. I sat in the middle of the lawn with

my head in my hands, rocking back and forth. The detectives

tried talking to me, but I wouldn't answer; I couldn't answer. I was in a state of shock. All in one year, I had lost two people that was dear to me.

"Come on. You have to get up from there," Melissa said, extending her hand.

I looked at her with my puffy eyes. "Just bury me here. Why was I even born? Why am I here? My life is cursed." I got up and walked towards the street. Flashbacks of my life kept repeating over, and over in my mind. The beaten, the raping, the prostitution, and the drugs. I wasn't as strong as I thought. My life was hopeless. Melissa stood and watched me with confusion.

"What are you doing, ma'am? There are oncoming cars that way," The officer yelled. I continued to walk into the street, picking up speed with every step.

"Claudia?!" Melissa yelled, as she raced to grab me. My life wasn't meaningful. Melvin was the only hope that I did have. He was the only reason that I gave my life back to Christ.

He was the only reason that I had faith in God anymore, and He took that away from me.

As I stepped into the road, a white SUV lifted me off of my feet. I heard faint yells in the back, as I felt my soul slipping away. I tried opening my eyes, but the light was too bright. There was a calmness that came over me. Something like I had never known before.

"Why are you here?" A male voice asked.

I looked around, as I covered my face. There was a bright light to my right, so bright that I could not make out the face. "I have no reason not to be. My life is over," I responded.

"It's not your time. There are some important things that you have to do. You have many people to help. This is all for a reason. You will soon understand. There is no destiny, without process. Go, and I will always be with you. My strength, is your strength.

"Claudia?! Claudia?! Come on baby; stay with us!"

Melissa yelled out. I began to cough, uncontrollably, as I

gasped for my breath.

"She's alive!" Melissa cried. The paramedics lifted me

up into the back of the ambulance and drove me to the hospital.

I had a broken leg, rib, and arm. It could have been a lot worst,

but that wasn't God's plan for my life. Even if I wanted to

leave, his plan is all that mattered. His glory. His will. His

purpose.

While laying up in the hospital I reflected over my life

and my near-death experience.

"Lord, have mercy on me," I cried out. I cried, I

screamed, I yelled, and I moaned. The nurse that was assisting

me walked into my room.

"Is everything okay?" She asked, worried, as she

checked the machines.

I shook my head. "My whole body is racking with pain. To know pain, is to live a life of pain and disappointments from a child. The horror that I faced, and the things that I had to go through, is something that you have never seen. And I wish for you to never see. I loss a whole lot, but I shall gain much," I said, as I wiped my face from the tears that flooded it.

"I don't know what you've been through, but I know that you have to be one strong cookie in order not to crumble. God has his hands on you," she said, as she placed new bags on the IV pole. I smiled and nodded. "Let me know if you need anything. I will be here all night. My name is Candace, which I wrote on the board. Just ring." She picked up her clipboard and exited the room. She must have slipped me some good meds, because the next thing you know, I was in la la land.

Chapter 13

The next morning, as I was opening my eyes, I saw faces; familiar faces. There was Melissa, Iyanna, and Pastor Cunningham, standing at the foot of my bed. I was so glad to see Iyanna alive and well. I smiled, but immediately, started to frown as I thought about Melvin. He wasn't here.

"Hey, sleepy head. How are you feeling this morning?" Iyanna asked, with a huge smile on her face. I took a deep breath and smiled, but seconds later, tears flooded my eyes like the Mississippi River.

"Give us a minute," Melissa told the Pastor.

"Very well," he said, as he exited the room. Iyanna grabbed my hand and began to cry.

"I'm so sorry sissy." She wept. Melissa stood next to Iyanna and rubbed her back.

"Now, now, we must stay strong for Claudia... for one another. God has brought us all together once again. Don't you see? We had to endure, but there was purpose in all of it.

Though Melvin has gone to be with the Lord, that doesn't change the profound affect that he left on each and every one of our lives. He had a mission to complete, and I truly believe that he completed it," she said, placing her hand on my head.

"Even though I may never understand God's way, I know that it's only for our good and His glory. All things are working for my good. All of our goods," I said, pointing with my one good arm. Pastor Cunningham came back in and prayed over our lives.

"Thank you, once again, for praying with us," Melissa said, as she walked pastor to the door.

"No, problem. You get well," he said, as he walked out the room. My sisters stayed with me until visitation was over.

Three weeks passed, and I was finally being released from the hospital. They had buried Melvin over two weeks ago, and his grave was my first stop. My heart was so broken that I wasn't able to make it to his funeral.

"You ready?" Melissa asked, as she escorted me into
the car.

We drove fifty miles outside of the city, where Melvin
was buried alongside his mother. My heart fluttered with hurt,
as I approached his grave. I made Melissa stop by the flower
shop to pick up white, red, and yellow roses. Red, for my
undying love, yellow for our friendship, and white for new
beginnings. I kneeled down at the gravesite and wiped my hand
across his grave. As the tears fell from my eyes, a sense of
peace blew across my face. I had to laugh, because I knew it
was Melvin. It was his way of letting me know that I could
finally live in peace and that he did not blame me for any of
that.

"I just want to let you know how much I love you. They
found your killers. Janice will pay for what she has done. I'm
learning to forgive, slowly, but surely. I just wish that you was
here with me. People say that, when someone passes on, they

are forever in their hearts, but I don't know if I can live with that. I guess I have no choice, though," I said, placing a rose on each side of his grave. "Rest, my sweet angel. I will forever miss you." Melissa walked up to me, placing her hand on my back.

"Are you ready?" She asked.

I nodded, "Yes…. yes."

Epilogue

One year later, they convicted Loco, Brick, and Janice of kidnapping, murder, attempted murder, and so forth. They were definitely not getting out anytime soon. Iyanna went off

to college in New York. She was studying to become a Lawyer.

Melissa and Gary were mending their marriage. Melissa said

that it was not easy, but it was worth it. Even though Gary was

a pain in the behind, he was perfect for Melissa. Besides, they

couldn't split up, because Melissa was expecting!

As for my mother, she moved into her own place and

had been clean for a whole year. Our relationship was getting

better, but it was still a little shaky. That was okay, because

there wasn't any more resentment or un-forgiveness. I loved

her from a distance. I was finally free. By me forgiving her, it

allowed her to forgive herself. She had also revealed that she

was molested when she was a very young girl, as well, and she

did not know how to deal with it in a positive way. Now, there

is finally a window where there were only walls. God was on

her side, and he was turning it around for her good.

As for me, well, I have never been happier. My spirit
has been cleaned and set free. I am no longer blind and can see
where God is directing me. He has replaced my hurt with joy. I
have traveled to different schools, group homes, homeless
shelters, etc. to speak to kids, or anyone that was brought up in
an abusive home. I speak to kids that have been abandoned,
wounded, and have lost love ones to violence. Through all of
my pain and all of my struggles, I have gained so much. Now, I
know why I had to go through what I went through. If I had not,
I wouldn't be prepared for my destiny.

I went back to school for Nursing, but I was also
studying ministry. You never know where your chaotic life will
bring you. As for Sam, he has changed his life completely
around. He is still in jail, but he has been an inspiration for
many locked up. He has two more years to serve. Hopefully, he
stays positive. I promise to serve God for the rest of my life,

because he has brought me from a mighty long way. I can't do

nothing less than give him the praise.

I visit Carrie's and Melvin's gravesite once a month. I

am forever grateful for Carrie, no matter the wrong she had

done behind my back. She was just as lost as me. My two best

friends were gone, but their legacy shall live on for eternity.

May their soul continue to rest in peace.

***

Even though the characters are fiction and this is not

about my life. It is about someone's life. There are so many

people that have suffered and has been set free. There are some

that are still suffering. Our actions in life can cause a deadly

future, but God sent his only Begotten Son to die for our sins

and the sins of our ancestors. We have the power to break off

the generational curses that are attacking us daily. I have

suffered... we all have suffered, in some way, but we don't

suffer to be crushed, we suffer to overcome. To gain, Claudia

was an example of a generational curse, but she had overcome

that curse and had broken every yoke that had her in bondage.

God knows our pain and all of our suffering. If you only

endure, he will bring you to your light.

***

"O you afflicted one. Tossed with tempest, and not

comforted. Behold, I will lay your stones with colorful

gems." Isaiah 54:11